Castle

Zombie Castle 3

Castle

Chris Harris

PRESS

Published by DHP Publishing in 2018
This edition published by Vulpine Press in the United Kingdom in 2025

Cover by Vulpine Press
ISBN: 978-1-83919-612-6

www.vulpine-press.com

CHAPTER ONE

Maud whistled loudly. The noise in the room subsided from the roar of laughter and conversation that had risen in volume as voices rose to be heard over the ever-growing racket.

We all smiled at the shocked look on Shawn's friends' faces as they stared in amazement that such a small and dainty looking old woman could whistle so loudly.

"This is all well and good, but I have children to feed and if you think I am cooking in that pigsty of a kitchen, you have another think coming."

She pointed to Ian.

"Shawn has told me about you. Apparently, you pride yourself in being the chief troublemaker, so I blame you for it. You have ten minutes to sober up and tidy the kitchen, or you will not be getting any food."

Silence descended as the big man looked around for help from his friends, who were staring at anywhere but in his direction. He looked at Maud. Seeing the determination in her face as she stood staring at him, hands on hips, he knew he had no other option and muttered.

"Yes, Ma'am. Can I take my armour off first, though?"

"Yes, but get on with it, we haven't got all day."

As soon as he and the others had helped each other remove their cumbersome attire, he dejectedly shuffled off to the kitchen.

1

Soon the rattle of pots and pans being cleared away could be heard, along with quiet muttering and curses.

Laughing, I spoke up.

"Right. Now you've met the true boss of our little group, we need to plan what our next move is. But first, we should catch up on what's happened to each other over the past few days."

"Too bloody right," said Dave. "Shawn, you bugger off on your own, leaving us to fight our way back here through thousands of zombies. Now you turn up with an armoured tractor, a Volvo that wouldn't look out of place in a Mad Max movie and everyone's got assault weapons and pistols. Also, if I am not mistaken, I'm sure I saw a bloody great machine gun being fired earlier. I think that our story isn't going to be anywhere near as interesting as yours."

Maud, once she had approved Ian's attempt at tidying, bustled around the kitchen making food for everyone from a bag she'd brought with her, as the two groups exchanged their experiences since the outbreak had started.

Simon and Dave were very interested in the weapons the knights used and the techniques for fighting that they'd adopted and adapted. Both agreed after handling the various axes, maces and swords leaning up against the wall, that with what both groups had learned from their experiences so far, their combined forces would present a formidable power: a combination of the peak of military weaponry design from different millennia, being used collectively to defend themselves from, and destroy enemies they were never designed to fight.

Shawn's friends examined and admired the firearms, but as none of them had any real experience in using them, Dave advised that until he could train them in their safe use, something he promised to do at the earliest opportunity, it would be best if they stuck to their medieval weapons.

They reluctantly agreed to this, but still cast envious glances over them and kept handling them until Dave pointed out that they were loaded and even though they were all 'safe', careless handling could result in a negligent discharge, which could result in tragic consequences. The guns got left alone after that.

Horace took a real shine to Sarah, who giggled as only a small child could as he nuzzled and licked her as she lay in the basket that had become her cot.

When everyone was hungrily tucking into the stew that Maud had made, I looked at my watch and said we needed to decide soon what we were going to do next. The idea of staying in a city teeming with the undead didn't seem the sensible thing to do, and as there were still a few hours of daylight left, I was keen for us to get moving again.

"This church you told us you were planning to head to. How long will it take us to get there?" Simon asked.

Jamie thought for a moment.

"Less than half an hour under normal circumstances. We know the way we came is clear of obstructions, and if we come across anything else, such as a pack of zombies, that tractor of yours, as you've already told us, will be able to break through. I reckon it should take an hour." His friends agreed with this estimate.

We began planning.

There was no doubt that it was best to use all the vehicles we now had at our disposal. The bus and the van both had different, but essential uses. The obvious ones being that the bus would enable us to accommodate more survivors when we found them, and both could carry a large amount of supplies.

Not being armoured, they'd also be the most vulnerable, so they'd need to travel in the middle of the convoy, with the tractor leading the way and the Volvo bringing up the rear.

Dave and Simon worked on a list for a few minutes and then got our attention.

Dave looked at Shawn's friends.

"I'll need one of you in the trailer to show Shawn the route, so if you can agree who that will be, I'd appreciate it. I'll put one or two shooters in your vehicles so if we get into trouble, even though I'm sure up close and personal you'll have no problems defending yourself, having a few guns on board won't do any harm. If some of you want to travel on the trailer, that would be great because a few extra strong arms on the zombie spears might be a great help. If you can sort that out between yourselves now, I think we should get moving as soon as we can."

To their credit, everyone wanted to travel in the trailer, as they realised it was where most of the fighting would probably take place.

Steve and Jim, as the trained Marines, were allocated to the bus and van respectively. Daniel volunteered to replace Steve in the Volvo while Jamie, Ian and Jon won the argument about who was going in the trailer.

Working with purpose, it didn't take long to repack the van and bus and clear the furniture that had been used to block the gaps.

The children's excitement at having to climb a ladder and walk across the roof of the bus to reach the safety of the trailer wasn't marred by the now familiar sight of more undead. They'd gathered outside, attracted by the noise we'd made, and replacing the ones we'd killed earlier.

The buoyant mood that everyone still felt since the groups had combined was enhanced further by Ian's attempt to climb the ladder and cross the roof of the bus while wearing his full suit of armour. His weight, along with the weight of the armour he was carrying proved too much for the thin roof, and to everyone's hilarity, his foot pierced it. It took four people, virtually helpless with laughter, and another pushing from underneath to pry him free. He eventually crawled ungracefully into the trailer, muttering and cursing about the quality of workmanship these days, but also smiling because he knew if it had happened to someone else, he would be leading the piss-taking.

Horace wanted to join his new master in the trailer, so instead of climbing aboard the bus, he too, comically tried to climb the ladder, eventually managing through sheer determination and a little help from others dragging and pushing him from behind, and to the delight of the children, he joined Ian in the trailer. He immediately forgot his new master though, as the fuss the children gave him proved a more worthwhile way for him to spend his time.

It took a few stern warnings about the dangers of the situation we were in to calm everyone down.

Once extra ammunition and weapons had been passed to Steve in the bus and to Jim in the van, we were ready to leave.

The starting of all four engines agitated the zombies surrounding the vehicles, as they seemed to realise that the meal they were hoping for was leaving.

With the passengers brandishing weapons, standing on seats and lining the sides of the trailer, Shawn ploughed the tractor through the throng that had gathered. We followed, setting out on what we hoped would be a short journey to the safety of the church in a small village.

Thirty people and one dog continued their journey.

CHAPTER TWO

Travelling closely together, the convoy followed Shawn through the streets of Bristol, spears continually thrusting at the shambling zombies that futilely tried to reach us in the safety of our vehicles.

Shawn maintained a speed sufficient to smash through every group of the undead that crossed our path. From my position in the rear, I couldn't see the devastation caused by the plough as it powered through the walls of bodies trying to stop us, but I could see the result. Dismembered and mangled bodies flew through the air; some remained still, but some continued thrashing about as the damaged caused hadn't destroyed the brain.

Unable to reach from their vehicles, the passengers in the bus and van were reduced to being mere witnesses to the effectiveness of what we had created.

As I drove, concentrating on keeping close to the van, I began thinking of how we would armour both the bus and the van. We had the skills and knowledge from what we'd done to my Volvo and the tractor, so the basics were obvious. The van would be easy. Add a wedge to the front and protect the driver's cab with whatever materials we could find.

The bus, though, was a different matter. Would we want it to be a transport vehicle or a fighting vehicle? Unless the windows were removed, there would be no way for the occupants to 'engage' zombies. Or would it be best to find enough steel mesh to encase it completely so the occupants would be protected, but would have to rely on others to keep the undead away? The bus, fitted with a strong wedge on the front, would have enough power and weight behind it to plough through zombies or to clear obstructions out of the way.

Up-armouring them needed to be one of our first priorities when we reached a place safe enough for us to do it. I was sure others were also thinking as I was, so most likely after today's journey, when we'd gained experience of how capable our little convoy was, the answers to my musings would be obvious.

The extra radios provided by Shawn's friends made communication between everyone easier. We could listen as Jamie gave Shawn directions and Louise, who was still travelling in the cab with Shawn, informed us all if any obstructions or zombies were ahead.

Louise's voice sounded through the radio.

"Stop, everyone. I saw something on the road we just passed."

Bringing up the rear, I'd stopped opposite the road she was talking about. I stood up on my seat and looked down it.

The road was a small cul-de-sac about one hundred yards long, lined with large post-war semi-detached houses. At the end of the road it widened to create the turning circle that surrounded a small grass island with a tree in the middle. Beyond the island, the front drive of one of the houses was engulfed with a mass of zombies.

I picked up the radio.

"Well spotted, Louise. Someone must be in the house down there."

I then asked the next question, even though I knew what the answer would be.

"If there are people down there, is everyone willing to take the risk to rescue them, even though we don't know them?"

I smiled as everyone confirmed that they and their travelling companions were more than willing to face the risks involved with trying to rescue others.

I looked at Dave, who was standing on the seat next to me looking through some binoculars.

"Your call, pal. Tell us what to do."

He looked for a few more seconds through his binoculars. "We can't all drive down there. It's too narrow, and we'll most likely block ourselves in like a bunch of idiots. I can see movement from the front first floor window, so I would agree that there's a good chance we have some live ones in there. The fact they're not waving and shouting at us may also be a good sign."

He paused, but didn't wait for me to question why before continuing.

"They must have seen and heard us by now. The fact that they're not drawing attention to themselves might mean they feel secure but are wary of who we might be. I take that to be a good indication that they're sensible and not some hysterical snowflake who expects us to fix everything for them.

"My suggestion is that we send Shawn in first. He can drive round and round the island at the end of the cul-de-sac, pulversing those bastards. We stay here to protect the bus and van until he's thinned them out enough for us to swap over to finish what he started. Then if he continues to protect the end of the road, with us providing covering fire, the bus can drive down and pick up whoever is in there."

I looked at him.

"Yep, I agree. Let's get on with it. We need to get to this church of theirs before night falls."

Dave quickly issued his instructions through the radio. As soon as Shawn confirmed he understood, he pulled forward, smashing through some front garden fences and hedges to turn his vehicle around, and with his engine roaring loudly, he gained speed as he hurtled down the narrow cul-de-sac.

I felt briefly concerned as I watched Becky wave at me from the trailer as it sped past. My wife and children were on the trailer that was once again leading the attack against a horde of flesh-eating monsters, while I watched from a distance. It was a catch 22 situation. The trailer was currently the safest zombie-proof vehicle we possessed. It was also the best vehicle we had for attacking them directly. Logically I would want my family as far away from danger as possible, but also in the safest place, and that was not possible.

At least the occupants of the trailer could bring a lot of fire-power to the party.

Shawn had made his first complete circle of the island before the zombies pressing up against the house started to turn in his direction. They moved towards the fast-moving target that was circling and just tempting them to attack it to get to the tasty flesh their senses told them it contained.

I was reminded of one of those machines that butchers have for slicing meat. Every pass Shawn made sliced the front from the solid mass of undead meat. The occupants of the trailer could only hold on as the trailer bounced and bumped over the growing pile of offal he was creating. I watched as the tractor under the influence of centrifugal forces lost traction on the slick of destroyed body parts. The trailer was also not dutifully following its master but skidding as its wheels slipped, causing the back of the trailer to smash through the ever-advancing pack. Shawn skillfully corrected the skid and kept the vehicle in a controlled power slide as it sped around the small turning circle.

Through Dave's binoculars I could see the smile on his face as he drove around what could only be described as the goriest skid pan ever created.

The trailer stopped outside the house after one more circle. As soon as it had, its occupants lined its sides and fired on the ones that had not been caught in the circling maelstrom of steel.

A call over the radio from Marc in the bus drew our attention away from the tractor.

"Got some zombies coming."

Dave looked along the road and saw a small group heading towards us in the direction we were going. He picked up the radio.

"Steve, Jim. You can deal with those. Get out of the vehicles and take them down when they're in range. Everyone else keep a good all-round lookout and call any more sightings."

Steve and Jim both stepped from the van and bus respectively and faced the oncoming threat.

I wasn't worried, the dozen or so approaching would be no match for the two Marines, but I also was aware that complacency could kill. Every threat needed to be taken deadly seriously.

Dave had the binoculars pointed back toward the house.

"The window's open upstairs. It looks as if they're talking to them."

Louise's voice came through the radio.

"The man and woman in the house are ready to come out. They'll wait for the bus to come down." Dave picked up the radio.

"Leave Jim and Steve protecting our rear. Marc, get ready to drive the bus down as soon as the trailer's clear. We'll lead the way. Stay alert, everyone. Remember you've got no guns now on the bus. Do not try anything stupid, we can cover you from the Volvo.

Shawn, when you're ready, get back up here and help Jim and Steve protect our backs."

Shawn didn't reply but waited for a final volley of shots from the trailer before he drove towards us at a much more sedate speed than he had entered the cul-de-sac with. As soon as he was clear, I pulled away down the road, Daniel, Chet and Dave standing ready with their weapons.

Marc reversed the bus back slightly and then drove forwards, following me closely. I stopped outside the house, leaving enough room for the bus to pull on the drive so it could get as close as possible to the front door, where we guessed the occupants would come from, and then I stood on the seat with my weapon held ready.

I could see Dave, Alex and Geoff standing at the front door of the bus, wearing full armour, weapons in hand. They looked a lot more terrifying than any fully armed modern soldier ever could. As the bus stopped, the door slowly hissed open. They stepped onto the field of carnage and immediately began swinging their weapons at the heads of corpses or remnants of corpses that lay close by and showed any signs of movement.

The sounds of firing echoed from the end of the road. "Come on!" I shouted, "we need to get going."

Geoff lumbered up to the front door and banged on it. It slowly opened, and a man and woman emerged, staring with wide eyes at the three knights who stood with their shields and weapons held ready. They both had rucksacks on their backs. The woman held a cricket bat in her hand and the man a felling axe.

A movement caught my eye. Three zombies appeared from the side of the house and started to head towards them.

Before I could shout a warning, Dave screamed. "Contact right," and raised his rifle.

The knights turned to face the threat. Geoff shouted at the two to board the bus and stepped forward with his mace held ready. He called to Dave,

"We've got this, save your ammo."

As the two people bustled onto the bus, the three knights spaced out and faced the approaching zombies.

Everyone in my car watched intently. This was the first time we'd seen the knights in action and I was keen to see how their weapons from a different age would perform.

Two more zombies had now appeared. Again, Geoff shouted, "Don't fire, we can handle this."

The three knights stepped forward with their weapons ready.

Dave and I kept our rifles aimed at the heads of the approaching zombies, fingers off the triggers, but ready to fire at a moment's notice if need be.

It was impressive to watch. All three attacked their chosen targets at the same time. Geoff's mace destroying the skull of one, it fell to the floor spilling brains on the driveway. Dave's powerful swing removed the head of another, to see it bounce across the lawn before coming to rest in a rose bush, while Alex thrust his sword at the face of the one approaching him. The razor sharp, heavy blade thrust at an upwards angle, entered through its mouth and burst out through the back of the skull. Killed instantly, its legs buckled, and he used the weight of it falling to pull the blade free.

In seconds, three zombies had been killed quickly and effectively. As soon as the first had fallen, though, they turned their attention to the two remaining ones. Dave's swing this time sliced through and removed the top of the nearest one's skull, while Geoff smashed his mace into the side of the last one's head with such force both its eyes popped out from the skull and dangled from the optic nerves as pulverised brains sprayed from the empty eye sockets.

The display over, the three knights wasted no time boarding the bus, the continuous firing from the end of the road a compelling indication that we needed to get moving again.

We were now thirty-two and a dog.

CHAPTER THREE

Dave picked up the radio as we drove back out of the cul-de-sac. "Shawn, get ready to move."

Shawn immediately replied, "Yep, I can see you coming. We're attracting a bit of a crowd here, so moving on would be good."

Getting closer, I could see everyone who could use a weapon, including Becky, firing over the side of the trailer. Jim and Steve stood between the trailer and the van, also firing. Reaching the end of the road, I could see the reason why. The road in the direction we had come from was now teeming with approaching zombies. The pile of corpses littered the ground in front of the mass, showing that the shooters were just managing to hold the advancing tide of death back.

Dave shouted to Steve and Jim to get back on board their vehicles. They both disengaged immediately and ran to the van and the bus, and as soon as the radios confirmed everyone was on board, Shawn pulled away. I waited for the bus and van to tuck in behind him, so I could resume my position at the rear of the convoy.

The firing stopped when Shawn started moving and the pack immediately began closing in. Even in the thirty seconds I had to wait for the convoy to form, I could see in my mirrors that the zombies were getting dangerously close.

Daniel, Chet and Dave waited, calmly standing on the seats of my car until those nearest were in range, before ending their existence with spear thrusts. As I sat there, waiting for the van to start moving, I realised how calm I was also feeling. The zombies weren't numerous enough yet to cause us any problems and as they were only behind us, I knew that as soon as Simon pulled away in the van, I would follow him and leave them in my wake.

The more zombies we killed, the more detached we all became from the act of ending the life of what had once been another member of the human race. It was a life or death situation and we currently had the upper hand. We were reasonably secure in an armoured vehicle we knew the capabilities of, and armed with a variety of weapons that could all end a zombie's life in one thrust, strike or trigger pull. Unless we became trapped by an unstoppable volume of them, we could always escape.

I didn't know what the future would bring, but for as long as we could stay alert and work together to keep one step ahead of the relentless enemy that most of the population of the United Kingdom had become, we stood a chance.

We continued driving.

The further we got out of the city, the fewer undead we came across and these were easily dealt with by Shawn either smashing through them or having their brains destroyed by a spear thrust.

As our new friends had promised, the road was clear. The evidence of obstructions that had been cleared, and dead and mangled corpses acting like a trail of breadcrumbs left behind, showed us we were on the right path.

The main road, as they had already told us from their earlier experience, did contain more zombies, the reasonably clear, wide

16

road acting as a funnel, channelling the undead towards the smoke still rising from Bristol. Shawn increased the convoy's speed, everyone trying to keep as close to the rear of the one in front as they could, and all relying on Shawn to use the weight and power of the tractor to clear the way. Louise kept up a running commentary to warn us if he was steering around any stopped vehicles, so we could keep following and maintain position as best we could.

I noticed, though, that when we had smashed through a crowd of them, the remaining ones turned and began shambling along after us, the target we provided far more tempting than the distant rising plumes of smoke.

Dave had also noticed this and, pointing his thumb behind him at the now following zombies said, "I think we'd better make sure that when we pull off this road to get to the church, none of this lot notices. The last thing I imagine we want to do is attract another horde."

"Yes, mate," I replied. "I don't think it's far now, so we can decide what to do when we get there."

Almost on cue, Jamie's voice came over the radio a few minutes later, advising Shawn that the turning we wanted was coming up on the left soon.

Louise's voice came back almost immediately, saying there was a small group of zombies gathered at the entrance to the road we needed to take.

Dave stood up on the seat and looked behind, back the way we'd come.

"The ones behind aren't in sight yet. We need to deal with the ones in front quickly and then maybe we'll be able to avoid them following us."

Daniel and Chet put down their zombie spears and grabbed their rifles. Dave, seeing this, turned to them.

"I think it'll be best if we go quiet for this one, lads." He picked up the radio.

"Listen, everyone. The ones that are following us are out of sight for the moment, but as we already know, they will keep going until they find us. We need to get rid of all the ones in front of us as quickly and quietly as possible and get down the lane, so they lose our trail. I want to do it quietly just in case there are any others nearby. We don't know how long we'll be staying at this church, so the fewer we attract can only be a good thing.

Shawn, see how many you can get with the tractor and then we'll finish them off from the Volvo. If you boys in the bus could get ready to kill any ones we can't get to, that would be a great help."

Dave's quick and accurate assessment of the situation and the tactical plan to deal with it made perfect sense and everyone quickly acknowledged they understood what to do and the convoy continued.

We stopped when told to by Louise. The three vehicles pulled alongside each other on the wide road to watch Shawn once again use his vehicle as our main weapon against the undead.

A group of about thirty zombies had herded together at the entrance to the lane we needed to take. Maybe they were the ones left behind when they'd led them away from the church a few days ago and somehow, they knew that human flesh was close by and hadn't joined the throngs heading towards Bristol, who must be continually passing as they were funnelled down the main road, following each other like lemmings.

They'd noticed us by now, and they started heading in our direction. Shawn waited until they were in the centre of the road before driving straight at and through them, spears thrusting from the trailer, claiming more as the plough on the front of the tractor pulverised them. He drove a short way and used the full width of the road and its grass verges to turn around and line up on the remaining ones, again thinning them out.

I saw him gesticulating from the cab and got the gist that he wanted me to have a go as he drove past us to turn around again.

With a shout of, "Get ready lads," I drove slowly into the remaining ones. Dave, Chet and Daniel soon dispatched the ones they could reach with their spears. I turned around and made one more pass, aiming the car at the last few in the road, bumping over the remains left by the tractor. If I could see one lying on the ground still moving, I tried to aim so my wheels would run over and crush its head. The weight added to my car with all the extra protection we had built onto it made this easier. When I got my aim right, you could feel the car rise slightly as it rode over the skull and then drop suddenly as the skull caved in and its brains spread over the road.

One or two were still untouched at the edges of the devastation we'd caused in only a few minutes. Dave picked up the radio and told the knights to get ready, but to be careful and make sure any they stepped over were already dead.

Pulling out of the way so I could turn around, Marc immediately drove the bus forward so the knights could get as close as possible to the few who were still staggering towards us.

To an outsider, it probably looked like a well-choreographed and practised manoeuvre, it was all done so smoothly. To me, it showed again how well we worked together. The two groups had both survived and fought against terrifying odds before we joined, and now combined, we were proving a formidable force who could easily work together.

Marc stopped the bus and the doors hissed open. With no hesitation, Dave, Alex and Geoff exited and took a few steps forward and ended the existence of the few remaining zombies. As soon as they hit the ground, they turned their attentions to the ones lying mangled around them, destroying the brains of any still moving, before turning and hurrying back on board.

Less than five minutes after Dave had issued his instructions and with Shawn leading the way, we drove down the narrow lane that led to the village.

As Dave sat back down in his seat, he summed up our performance.

"Fuck me. I have never seen such unit cohesion from a bunch of FNGs before."

"FNGs?" I asked.

"Fucking New Guys. We're operating as if we're bloody special forces or something, not a load of civvies driving around in bastardised Mad Max vehicles, including some chaps who like to dress up and pretend they're King bloody Arthur. I doubt if I had the best of all the Marines I've trained in my whole career, that we'd be doing as well as we are."

I chuckled, "I think you're probably right, mate. But this isn't some training exercise or even a battle, where if one of us gets hurt we can call for immediate support and medevac. We're fighting together as a family where we don't get any second chances. We have no back-up apart, from each other. If a mistake is made, one or all of us dies. It's as simple as that.

"And that's what's making the difference, I think. I would do anything without hesitation to protect my wife and children, as would anyone else in this group, I imagine. But yes, I do agree the way we have and are getting through this is remarkable. Never in my wildest dreams could I imagine us doing what we're doing. Not many days ago I was shitting myself, screaming in absolute terror as I tried to escape from the camp site we were on, thinking we wouldn't even survive the next hour. Now, I must admit I'm reasonably positive about our chances, and I really think that if things carry on the way they *have* done, we've got a chance to eke out some existence from all this shit that's happening around us."

"I bloody hope so, mate. Something or someone made sure we all got together. It would be a damn shame if we wasted the opportunity by getting ourselves eaten."

He stopped talking and stood up on the seat again.

"I can see the spire on the church, it can't be far now." He looked back at Chet and Daniel, who were also sitting down. "On your feet lads, it looks as if we're getting close."

As Jamie gave Shawn the last few directions, the atmosphere in the vehicle tensed.

What would we find? A few days ago, eleven people had been in the church. They were in a secure place and had enough food to last for some time, with no need to leave the sanctuary they had sought shelter in. But a lot could happen in a few days and sometimes fate didn't not play fair.

Louise's voice came over the radio as we entered the village green, telling us it all looked clear. It was a very picturesque place, a typical English village green, the church dominating the skyline with the pub facing it. The rest of the green was lined with pretty houses of all shapes and sizes.

It was one of those places you liked to drive to for a Sunday lunch or maybe a drink on a warm summer's day. As you sat on the bench in the pub garden, you would look around and say to yourself it was where you wanted to live and then reach for your phone to check out properties for sale in the area. You would then wistfully look at houses you just could not afford before finishing your drink or your meal and driving back to real life.

On close inspection though, the abandoned cars littering the road, the barricade of vehicles blocking the entrance to the church yard and the corpses I could see lying by the church doors, shattered the rural idyll the village used to portray. It was quiet and peaceful, but it had an air of abandonment and panic.

The vehicles stopped in a line, facing the vehicular entrance to the church that Shawn's friends had told us they had helped to block, using abandoned cars left by their owners as they fled the chaos of the first day of the apocalypse.

A few zombies that had been shambling around aimlessly started to head in our direction. Before anyone could ask, the doors to the bus opened once more and the three knights stepped down, quickly dispatching the nearest ones. A couple more were further away so they stood ready, waiting for them to get closer.

While they were waiting, a shout from the church steeple made us look up. A man was leaning over the parapet, waving.

Ian shouted up from the trailer. "Bob, is that you? We told you we'd be back, we've brought some new friends along. If you wait while we deal with the last few heading towards us, then we will clear the barricade and get inside."

The man high up on the steeple shouted he understood and disappeared from view, most likely descending the tower to come and meet us.

Knowing the last few zombies approaching would pose no problem to the knights, I climbed out of the Volvo and went to the trailer to steady the ladder Simon was lowering.

Good old Maud. I didn't need to say anything to her. She was standing, looking over the side of the trailer at approaching zombies, cradling Sarah in her arms. As soon as I saw a child's hand touch the ladder, she said softly,

"Now children, let's wait up here until we get inside the churchyard. Then you can get down and help everyone. I need you to stay up here and help protect Sarah and me."

Even though I couldn't see my children, I heard a chorus of slightly reluctant agreements as they made way for the adults to descend the ladder.

We had a strange balance to work out between protecting the children at all costs, sheltering them from the constant horror we were experiencing, and preparing and training them to survive in the world we now lived in.

I'd seen Stan and Eddie lining the trailer sides, using a zombie spear to kill as many as possible when driving through a throng of them, but also in the same day playing tig in the yard at Willie's farm, running around laughing and carefree. Basically, being children.

Their normal childhood had ended the second the outbreak happened, and they did need to be trained on how to kill them and to survive, as we all did. But I still felt better if they could be kept out of harm's way whenever possible. The trick was to manage that, but still make them feel they were contributing to the group and part of the team we'd become. If they felt too overprotected, they might try something rash which could end in tragedy.

We wasted no time and started to push the vehicles away from the entrance. Dave asked a few to maintain perimeter security and to back the knights up if need be, while everyone else helped move the barricade. The many willing hands soon cleared the way and the vehicles drove up the drive towards the church. Again, with no prompting, the convoy positioned itself to protect the main church doors. Jamie left the van back slightly, so he could block the final gap when everyone had entered the church.

In the silence following the engines being turned off, the only sound was the squealing of protesting hinges as the ancient church doors opened.

Blinking in the bright sunlight, the inhabitants of the church filed out to meet us.

We now numbered forty-three and a dog.

CHAPTER FOUR

The last few visible zombies had now been killed by the knights and they were walking towards the church.

"It's great to meet you," I said to the group from the church. "I'm Tom. If we can first of all get the cars back over the entrance, we can all meet properly then."

One of them stepped forward.

"Yes, absolutely. I'm Jim and I'll introduce the rest later, but you're right. Let's secure the place."

He then turned to Ian and chuckled.

"Bloody hell, mate, I know you said you'd try to come back, and I was really hoping you would, but never in my wildest dreams did I ever imagine this. You lot have really got your shit together."

Then I noticed the two we'd picked up earlier. They were standing slightly separate from everyone else and still looked in shock from all that had happened to them today. In all the excitement of reaching the church and now that the group had grown so large, they had inadvertently been forgotten. I walked over to them to rectify our mistake as the rest walked down to the entrance gates.

"Hi, I'm Tom," I said, holding out my hand. "Sorry about not including you then, it's all a bit crazy at the moment, as you can imagine."

They both shook my hand and the woman spoke.

"Oh, it's okay. I'm Nicky and this is my husband Chris. We're just trying to take it all in. We thought we were done for until we heard and then saw you drive past. I can't describe the relief we felt when you stopped and came to rescue us, we just can't thank you enough. The guys on the bus have filled us in a bit on what you've been up to and it all sounds incredible."

"I know what you mean. When we tell the story ourselves, we can hardly believe it, but here we are. Anyway, if you want to come and help us move those cars back, we can get a brew on and get to know each other better."

They agreed, and we walked down to help the others.

Twenty minutes later, when we were all satisfied that the churchyard was secure again, we helped Maud and the children down from the trailer and trooped into the cool interior of the church.

The church looked very organised. A cooking area had been set up and the pews arranged to make a large communal seating area. One wall was lined with what looked like a sleeping area, with areas divided by blankets hanging off ropes to provide an element of privacy.

The church was everything they'd told me it would be. It provided a safe and secure refuge, with the bonus that the perimeter wall should keep all but a huge mass of the undead out.

As everyone sat down on the pews, I did notice that the three different groups, us, the knights and the church occupants, sat together. At first, the two new additions looked unsure where to sit, before sitting near to Marc, who had been driving the bus. I was sure a psychologist would see it as an interesting study on society and the bonds that people formed even after a short time together. Tribal could be another way to describe it. The three separate groups had worked together to survive and so the bonds they felt would be stronger than feelings towards the other groups. Shawn was the exception. He had the recent emotional contact with us, but also a strong, much longer-term emotional attachment to the friends he had lived with for years. He did choose, though, to sit with our group next to Louise, who he had spent the last few days in the tractor cab with.

I wasn't sure what the intentions of the church group were yet, but as Shawn's friends were joining us on our journey, the two groups would quickly and easily merge into one strong unit; our survival depended on it.

The vicar had remained standing as we all sat down, and he took the lead now. He walked into the centre of the seating area and the chatter that had begun died down. He spread his arms in a universal welcoming gesture.

"Welcome, everyone. I can't say how much pleasure it gives me to welcome old friends and new to the sanctuary my church has become."

He turned to the group of knights.

"Without your help, I doubt any of us would have survived and now you've brought many new friends and some amazing looking vehicles. I'm desperate to know your story, just as I'm sure everyone else must be. But first, let us offer you some refreshments and food to officially welcome you."

With that, he went and shook our hands in turn and blessed everyone with the sign of the cross.

Becky whispered to me, "I'll go and see if they have enough supplies, it's not fair to use theirs when we have so much."

I squeezed her hand and replied, "Good idea, love."

As Becky walked away, Dave called me over.

"I think we need to set an OP up in the spire." I looked quizzically at him.

"Sorry. An Observation Post. I'll ask that guy over there, I think he said his name was Jim. He's one of the coppers, I believe, so I imagine he's their security expert. One person on watch at a time should do it and now there are so many of us, the rota won't be hard to organise. Do you think the children will be up for it too?"

"Good idea, mate. I imagine they were doing it anyway. There was someone up there when we arrived, after all. Come on, let's go and have a chat with him."

Jim told us what they'd been doing for the past few days. They had kept a constant watch from the tower. Until more of the undead had started to drift into the village, they'd managed to scavenge some more supplies from neighbouring houses. Erring on the side of caution, they'd then retreated to the church and kept as quiet as possible. This worked and most of the zombies had shambled away, just leaving the few that we'd dealt with when we arrived.

Dave called to Jim, the Marine, and told him to grab a radio and go and take the first watch in the Spire, promising to send up some food and drink when it was ready.

With a, "Yes, boss," he picked up a radio and his weapon and after a quick comms check to make sure the radios were working, followed the other Jim, who showed him the way to the Spire.

Becky had, with the help of a few others, unloaded some of our supplies from the trailer and was helping in the cooking area. The children had gathered in the area of the church that contained children's books and games and were happily amusing themselves. They'd even taken baby Sarah off Maud and were playing with her on the carpet of the 'play area'.

Maud, never one to sit still or take a break, was bustling around, and was introducing herself to all the church occupants. The smile on her face was infectious and her bubbly spirit and personality were a tonic everyone seemed to enjoy.

Again, I thought about how Maud had changed from the cowed, bullied woman who was unable to speak for herself when we first met her, to the woman she had become today. She was the matriarch of the group, constantly looking after the welfare of all of us, especially the children, and never afraid to put any of us in our place if we overstepped the invisible lines of behaviour she expected.

Then I silently chuckled to myself. It wasn't surprising really, seeing as her first act had been to hack her bullying, cowardly worm of a husband to death with a hand axe when he had tried to push her in the way of an approaching zombie horde to save himself, telling her she must die to save him.

Soon everyone had a bowl of food and a hot drink in their hands and we all began retelling our stories, with others chipping in if they thought something had been missed. The laughter and tears that we all shed at various parts of each other's stories bound the groups together more as the experiences of each group were now the shared experiences of the whole group.

Chris and Nicky's story was one none of us had heard yet, so once they had listened, laughed and cried at all our exploits, everyone quietened down to hear their tale.

The main news was that Nicky was pregnant and that was what most likely saved their lives. They both worked in Bristol. Chris was a manager at a local Builders' merchant and Nicky was a corporate lawyer based at the Bristol office of a national firm, and they had taken the day off work to go to the hospital for the first scan of their unborn child.

The appointment wasn't until midday, so they had an easy morning pottering around the house and spending time together, excitedly biding the time until they could see an image of their first child. They hadn't listened to the news or radio, so they had no idea what was going on until they tried to leave their road. The lack of traffic and the abandoned cars littering the road immediately made them realise that something was seriously amiss, but nothing was going to stop them getting to the hospital, so they continued with their journey.

It wasn't until Nicky turned the radio on in the car that they both heard the government issued message. They stopped and tried to work out if it was some elaborate hoax and they'd suddenly see TV cameras and a presenter shouting, "Gotcha!" as he shoved a microphone in their faces, or if it was true.

Even when a blood and gore covered thing approached the car and started clawing at its windows, they discussed calmly whether it was real or a very good make-up job. It was only when another approached, whose both arms were bloody stumps, and it began banging its head against a window, breaking all of its teeth in the effort, that they came to the panicked realisation that it must all impossibly be true.

Chris slammed the car into reverse, smashing into a few cars in his terrified efforts to escape, and they tried to make it back to the safest place they could think of.

Their home.

Driving as fast as he could, they swerved through the streets, dodging cars and zombies apparently in greater numbers now that the secret was out. They almost made it until they were stopped by a horde blocking the way ahead.

With more coming from behind them, they had no choice but to abandon their car and run for it, dodging through gardens and alleyways until they reached their house, just closing the front door before the ones that had appeared in their road reached them. As the crowd gathered outside, they realised that escape was impossible, so all they could do was barricade themselves in and wait. Hoping that they might get the chance to escape at some point, they filled rucksacks with as many useful supplies as they could, worked out what items they had round the house would be the best weapon, and tried to eke out their food supplies for as long as they could.

Day after day, though, the zombies gathered at the front of their house did not disperse but worse still, more arrived. Chris and Nicky had almost resigned themselves to never escaping, and facing the agony of starving to death in their own house, made worse by the knowledge that they would never see their unborn child and it would die with them, when the convoy had spotted and rescued them.

As soon as they had finished their tale, the women rushed to Nicky to congratulate her on being pregnant, and noisily began discussing the best care plan, so they could keep her and her unborn child as safe and well as possible.

Escaping from the women, Chris walked over to me. "Congratulations, mate," I said, shaking his hand. "I think your wife will be the best cared for lady in this world we're living in." Laughing as I thought of it, I added.

"I've just realised, you lucky bastard. Whatever happens, you're going to be guaranteed the comfiest bed available every night. No one's going to let a pregnant woman sleep on the floor if there's a bed available."

Ian whispered theatrically to Shawn and nodded over in Louise's direction. "Mate, if you get your new girlfriend preggers, don't worry I'll let her share my bed. You can sleep on the floor while I look after her. Anyway, you haven't told us what's going on yet. You bugger off, leaving us to get on with it on our own and then eventually turn up with a really hot woman, who is way out of your league, by the way. Then you don't come and sit with us, your mates, who've looked after you for years but sit cuddling up next to her."

Ian stood back, folded his arms and waited for an answer.

Shawn went bright red with embarrassment and stammered his reply.

"She's not my girlfriend. It's not like that. We're just friends, that's all. She'd just lost her sister and I just wanted to be there to help her."

His friends stood around him, waiting for him to continue. But he didn't, he just stood there looking for a way to escape.

Ian grabbed him in a bear hug, lifted him up and shouted. "Bugger me, boys, he's actually fallen in love."

Then he spun him around while Shawn tried to get him in a headlock and cover his mouth as he chanted like a child, "Shawn's in love!" over and over.

All the men found this infantile display very funny and laughed at the embarrassment it was obviously causing.

Glancing over at Louise, I could see she'd also gone bright red and was trying to hide her embarrassment too – and the big smile that had spread across her face.

Maybe Ian was right. It took a sharp shout from Maud to stop the merriment.

"Ian! Do I have to keep telling you to behave? You may have got away with this behaviour before and think you can get away with again it, because you are a big cuddly bear of a man with a permanent stupid grin on his face. Sarah is sleeping and if you have woken her with your stupid goings on, there will be hell to pay."

Instantly contrite, it was his turn to go red with embarrassment as he gently put Shawn down and muttered, "Sorry, Maud."

"And so you should be. Now go over and wash those dishes. They won't do themselves, will they?"

Once again Maud had got it spot on. The men, trying to stifle the laughter that wanted to erupt from our throats, watched as Ian dejectedly shuffled off and began washing the dishes like a severely scolded five-year-old.

He'd finally met his match in a sixty-year-old diminutive woman who looked as if she wouldn't say boo to a goose.

We knew differently.

We were still forty-three and a dog.

CHAPTER FIVE

We needed to get down to business and plan what our next move would be. Dave, Jim and I got everyone to gather at the seating area so we could begin.

I spoke first. "You all know of our plan to head to Warwick Castle and I still think we should stick to that goal. Unless anyone else has a better idea?"

No one indicated they did, so I continued.

"Of course," I said, looking at our newest arrivals, "you're all welcome to come with us, unless you prefer to stay here or have somewhere else you want to try to reach. But from what we've seen out there and with what goodies we've gathered so far, my firm belief is that your best and safest option will be to join us, so we can work together to survive all this shit that's going on around us."

No one spoke up, but I could tell from the looks on their faces that they knew joining us was the best option to ensure their survival.

"What we need to do now is plan the next few days. The main priority is, I imagine, working our magic on the bus and the van.

We know what we've done to the other vehicles works, so if a few of you can get thinking about those, that would be great. You locals can help with that, because you might know the best place where we can get the stuff we need.

Remember, we're still going to try and see if Louise's family in Cheltenham made it. From here, it's not far to them at all, and also, let's not forget Steve's family in Worcester. Time is of the essence for both those tasks, so whatever we do, we need to get on with it.

"If anyone else has people they want to check on, tell us now so we can try and plan the route to them. No promises of course, but if we can, we will try."

I stopped and looked around.

"Does anyone else have anything they want to add?"

Simon Wood stood up.

"Yes, mate. While you're tinkering with the vehicles, I want to work on tactics for fighting them. I've seen the way the knights fight, and it's frikkin' awesome. But I think that because we hope to try to rescue others on our way, we'll most likely be doing close quarter work and house clearing. Warwick castle, when we get there, might also be overrun.

We're heavily trained in urban warfare, so it's something the four Marines here are good at. But we need more than the four of us doing it. I think a couple of hours knocking our heads together will be a great help. Also, looking at the weapons you knights have, the rest of us are going to need something better than knives for close quarter work."

I nodded and looked around.

"Great idea. If you can get on with that, we can rotate round jobs, so we can all have a go. The training you've given us so far has, as we know, enabled us to work well together, even though we are FNGs."

He nodded, smiling, and sat down. I could see from the few quizzical expressions I would have to explain what FNGs meant. Once the children were out of earshot, of course.

The vicar was the next to stand.

"Even though it will break my heart to leave my parish, I don't think our future lies here. You have, as far as I am concerned, been sent here by God to be our guardian angels and my place is with you. I can't speak for the rest of the villagers, but I imagine they feel the same. This church has provided us with safety and sanctuary, but for how long? I've visited Warwick Castle, so I know it could provide all we need."

Bob stood up and interrupted him.

"I'm sorry for interrupting, Vicar, but I can speak for us all here and we all agree that we can't stay here long term. We'd eventually run out of food, and with so few of us, we just haven't got the strength to fight them off if we get surrounded again. Our best option is to leave with our new friends and survive this together."

"Thank you, Bob," replied the vicar, who turned to face us again.

"Well there's your answer. I am not sure, apart from the two police officers, what skills we can offer, apart from a willingness to help, but thank you for allowing us to join you. Now, if you can tell us how we can help, we will do our utmost not to let you down."

Chris stood up next.

"I have no doubt either that joining you is the best thing to do. We already owe you our lives. I'm not sure what I can add to the skillset apart from my years working in a builders' merchants, helping builders plan and design jobs and getting over the many problems that entails, and it goes without saying, a willingness to do anything to protect my wife and unborn child."

As he sat down, I continued, "Well, thank you, all of you."

The church was darkening as the sun sank lower in the sky, indicating another day survived.

"It's getting too late to go on a supply run to get more materials for the vehicles, but it won't stop us planning and getting ready for the morning. If we can get started on a few jobs now, we can make the most of tomorrow."

The noise level increased as everyone stood and started talking.

Simon and Dave came over and said the first thing they would do was start firearms training with all the new arrivals. With the help of Shane, they unloaded more weapons from the trailer and began splitting up the new trainees into groups to begin the basics.

The knights and the villagers were soon listening intently as they were shown safe handling discipline.

I couldn't help but chuckle at the sight of the vicar wearing his cassock holding an assault rifle, practising inserting and ejecting a magazine. How the world had changed!

Becky had gathered a few people and they were clearing an area to extend the sleeping space, enabling it to accommodate us all.

No one was idle, everyone had found a job to do and was getting on with it.

Shawn and I went outside to start planning the alterations to the vehicles and to draw up a list of materials we would need. We had plenty of tools and the generator to power them. The van, as I had thought earlier, was easy to plan. We just needed to add the ubiquitous and proven wedge to the front and protect the driver and passenger in the cab with mesh, if we could get it, or sheeting with holes cut in it to provide vision.

The bus, on the other hand, gave us more options to consider. We could simply add a wedge and protect all the windows, but that didn't give the occupants the ability to fight any zombies from the safety of being on board.

The bus would provide a more comfortable place for the large group we now had to travel in, but if for some reason it became separated from the main convoy, the occupants would need to be able to defend themselves.

After playing around with a few ideas, the best solution we came up with was to cover all the windows with bars or mesh but to remove the glass from every other window and the seats by them to create an area where they could fight from, either with guns or spears.

If it didn't work, we could always change it. The one thing we both agreed was essential, was to cut an escape hatch in the roof on both vehicles. In the fading light we unloaded the tools we would need and started to cut holes in various places on the bodywork of both vehicles, so when we got the materials we could begin immediately.

The children were already asleep when darkness and exhaustion finally drove us inside.

Keeping the noise down as much as we could, we barricaded the church door for the night and settled down in the pews. The flickering of candles provided enough light for everyone to see each other and to get around without tripping over anything, but most importantly, not waking the sleeping children.

Bottles of wine and beer were opened, and the group sat around enjoying each other's company, before tiredness and the need for an early start reminded us of the need for sleep.

Forty-three people, with regular lookout changes, and a snoring dog, slept soundly.

CHAPTER SIX

The early dawn light streaming through the church windows woke me and a few others up and we gathered in the kitchen area, quietly grumbling about the early hour and drinking the first coffee of the day, as one by one we were joined by more bleary-eyed adults who, too, seemed unwilling to communicate much until they had a mug of steaming tea or coffee in their hands.

Eventually, everyone had had a drink and some breakfast, and we felt ready to start the day.

Bob told us told us there was a farmer's supply warehouse in a nearby village that should provide us with all we would need to work on the vehicles, so Simon and Dave quickly planned the mission.

Dave and Jim would remain behind to continue weapons training, while Simon took Dave's place next to me in the Volvo. Shawn would, as usual, be driving the tractor, with Louise to accompany him. Both looked pleased at the news.

Simon then explained that he wanted to take some of the knights with us, but the problem would be mobility. Wearing a heavy suit of armour would make it difficult and slow to climb up and down the ladder to get in and out of the trailer. Not only would they enhance our fighting capabilities greatly, but also, they were the youngest and probably the fittest amongst us, and if we had to load a quantity of heavy material onto the trailer, then it made sense for them to be there.

Shawn spoke up.

"I was thinking about this last night, Simon. Watching Ian failing to get into the trailer when we left Bristol got me thinking. The rear of the trailer hinges from the side but the locking bar is on the outside. If I make one for the inside, it would be easy enough to make a ramp that we could drop in place. Then it would be a lot easier for everyone to get in and out and make loading stuff on a lot better too. If I can get it right, we could get a lot of fighting men on the ground quickly."

Simon thought about it for a moment. "How long will it take you?"

"Half an hour to rig something up, and I can improve it later."

"Good, you have twenty minutes! Right, then. While Shawn's doing that, can we all muck in and clear the trailer to make space for what we hope to get? When we get back, we'll need to distribute all the ammunition and other goodies we got from the soldiers the other day.

Shawn, can we also give some thought to how we mount the light machine guns we've got to the trailer, and possibly the Volvo too. If we get those right, the amount of fire we can accurately put down could be a game changer if we get into deep shit."

The large quantity of rifles and shotguns, military and sporting that we'd collected from both Bickley Barracks and the gun shop, along with the huge amount of ammunition we'd amassed from both places, and from the soldiers we'd met on the M5 motorway, made a truly impressive sight when it was stacked in the cool interior of the church. But would it be enough to keep us safe?

Shawn, true to his word, had drilled some holes in the trailer and made a crude but effective locking bar that would enable the rear of the trailer to be opened from within. With the Vicar's permission he'd also used the wood from a couple of pews to make a ramp. He'd designed a simple but clever system of ropes to get it on and off the deck of the trailer. If you pulled the ropes one way it extended out and dropped to the ground and if pulled in the opposite direction with a little more effort, it lifted it back onto the deck.

Using the theory that if it could take his weight, it could take anyone's, he got Ian, wearing full armour, to climb up it to see if it worked.

Grumbling about, "Getting the fat boy to try it first," Ian tentatively climbed up the ramp.

It creaked and sagged in the middle but held his weight.

When he reached the top, he got us all laughing as he performed a little victory dance, which in his armour looked more like he was having a fit.

We were ready to go then, so Simon quickly got everyone else he'd chosen to come on the mission on board both the trailer and the Volvo, and we waited while the ones staying behind cleared the barricade of cars out of the way.

Only Bob joined us from the newest additions to the group, because he knew the way. We explained to the others that because they hadn't had enough experience fighting from the trailer, or any training using the zombie spears, that they shouldn't come.

Besides that, they needed more training to use the guns, and thankfully, they understood and saw the sense in it.

We hoped this mission wouldn't take too long, and space was at a premium because we were also hopeful we'd be loading a large quantity of supplies, so every person we took along needed to be the most competent we had.

Shawn already had directions from Bob, but if we had to change from the pre-planned route, then Bob's local knowledge would be vital.

With a final wave, we left the church.

Shawn drove over the one or two zombies that had wandered into the village green overnight on our way out of the village. You couldn't hear their moans over the noise of the engines, but their lives ended abruptly again as they futilely tried to stop our progress by walking in front of the blood-smeared plough attached to the bucket on the tractor. What was left of them banged against the wedge at the front of my vehicle when they emerged from under the trailer's wheels.

The farmers' supplies was on the edge of another village and had obviously not opened on the morning the apocalypse had hit. The gates to the yard were still locked and the place looked deserted.

Simon quickly climbed down from my car and using a pair of bolt croppers, cut the chain locking the gate and slid them open to allow us to drive into the yard, closing it behind us.

Before allowing us to disembark from both vehicles, he and Steve did a full check of the area before declaring it clear of the undead.

I could see from my vantage point standing on the seat of my car that the large yard, with its neat stacks of timber, fencing and all the paraphernalia that a farmer needed to manage his land and livestock, was a treasure trove that would provide us with everything we would need and more.

When everyone gathered together, we started work; everyone apart from Louise, whom Simon had told to stay on the tractor to stand guard for us.

The forklift truck, sitting in an open-sided shed, would make loading a lot easier, but the key was predictably not in the ignition. It was almost certainly going to be locked in an office in the warehouse and sales counter located in a corner of the yard, so three of us grabbed the bolt cutters and went to break open the shutters securing it.

The skylights provided enough light inside for us to see around, once we'd pulled the shutter open and used a sledgehammer we got from the trailer to smash the door open. Easily finding the keys that were on a hook in the manager's office, we took them outside to help load up.

Simon was standing next to a Land Rover Defender 110 that was in the livery of the company we were in the process of robbing. He was trying the door, but it was locked.

I knew exactly what he was going to say, so I said it for him. "I'll go and look for the keys, shall I?"

He nodded with a big grin on his face and pointed to a large twin axle trailer next to it.

"We just found ourselves a new scout vehicle, and if we hook that baby up, we can take a lot more stuff back with us too. If we can work our magic on that too, it'll give that Chelsea tractor of yours a run for its money."

"Leave my bloody Volvo out of this will you, it's got us this far, hasn't it?" I said as I walked back into the warehouse to find the keys.

The keys still had the Land Rover key ring on them, making them also easy to find. Walking back through the shop, I could see that we needed to take a lot of things that were stored in there too.

The shelves were full of hand tools that would make great zombie killers and boxes of screws, bolts and other fittings that would probably make constructing our Mad Max style vehicles easier.

Then I noticed a small sign above the sales counter, informing customers that shotgun licences must be shown for cartridge purchases.

"Brilliant," I thought as I went searching for the place where they stored them.

The heavy-duty locked door at the back of the manager's office proved no match for the long crowbar I took from the shelf. It revealed a large quantity of shotgun cartridges of all weights. Mainly in 12 gauge, but I spotted a few other gauges too.

We had to take them as a priority. Walking outside, I handed Simon the keys to his prize Defender and told him I needed two others to help so we could start emptying the shop too.

The forklift was making the job of loading up a lot quicker and easier than expected. Simon agreed and told Chet and Bob to go with me. Grabbing a trolley each, I gave them a quick idea of what to grab as I headed with my trolley to the manager's office.

Chet and Bob both did a male version of the hit 90s game show, Supermarket Sweep, loading their trollies with axes, hammers and pickaxes and a plethora of other tools, grabbing armfuls off the racks and dumping them in the trollies as fast as they could before running to the next item they spotted. I took mine to the cartridge store and began to clear that out too.

When the trollies were full, we pushed them as quickly as we could and dumped their contents first in the back of the Volvo, and when that was full up, into the back of the Land Rover.

I couldn't help myself as I dragged the theme tune from deep in my memory and began to sing it loudly as we continued to fill the trollies. Chet and Bob joined in as they charged around the shop, banging the heavily overloaded trollies off shelves as they failed to make the corners.

Once I'd cleared all of the cartridges from the store, I joined the other two and loaded anything else I could see that was worth taking. From dog food for Horace to work boots and coats, we threw everything we could into the trollies.

Simon, meanwhile, had hooked up the trailer to the Defender and was driving it around the yard, loading as much as he could onto it.

I took him some tie-down straps I'd taken off a shelf, so he could secure the load properly when he'd finished.

We were dripping with sweat and exhausted from all the running around and heavy lifting, but we had done amazingly. Within an hour, we had gathered more materials to armour the vehicles than we needed and had gathered more supplies that would be essential to our ongoing survival.

Another successful trip, but a shout from Louise drew our attention to the fence surrounding the yard. The noise we'd been making had attracted some unwelcome attention. Zombies were beginning to line the fence surrounding it and we could see more coming. Their simple brains couldn't distinguish between a fence and the main gate. Most of them just pressed futilely against the steel mesh fencing, thrashing their arms against the barrier, biting it in their frustration at knowing we were there but being unable to reach us. A few were at the gate, pushing at it, making it rattle on its runners.

None of us was too concerned. The gate and fences were strong enough to hold them back and we were almost done and would be on our way back before the numbers grew to the level that could cause the fence to be compromised.

Still we decided to err on the side of caution and call it a day. We'd taken more than we needed, and the real work would start when we got it all back to the church. I helped Simon finish strapping down the load to his trailer and then helped the trailer occupants lift the ramp back into place and close the rear door. They had loaded so much onto it, they were almost standing level with the top of the sides and were busy jamming lengths of timber down the sides to try to hold the load steady when they were moving.

Simon and I agreed as we finished strapping the trailer that it would be best for him to travel as the middle vehicle in the convoy, where the two armoured vehicles could help protect him if need be. Common sense, really, but planning ahead had got us to where we were now.

Chet was the last to climb into the Volvo. I could see that by now between fifteen to twenty zombies were clawing at the gate. We had no time to waste, the priority was to get back to the church as quickly as possible, so we could start adapting the vehicles. I picked up the radio.

"We haven't got the time to mess about and deal with those buggers at the gate by hand. Shawn, stay where you are, we'll deal with them from the car. Once the gate is open, drive through and cover us as we close it."

Louise came back immediately. She'd become the tractor's official radio operator, leaving Shawn to concentrate on driving the Behemoth.

"No probs, Tom, be careful."

Pulling up to the gate, I stopped at an angle, facing it, and the three of us stood. Simon was now driving the Land Rover. He was adamant that he didn't want anyone riding shotgun for him as the vehicle didn't have any protection on it yet and it would only put someone else in possible danger.

We picked up our rifles and took aim. The red dot sights and the range, virtually point blank, made it easy for us. With each shot another zombie fell back from the gate, its head a mess of oozing blood and brains. As soon as the last one fell, Steve jumped down and slid the gate open.

Attracted by the noise and movement, every zombie lining the fence and heading towards it started to shamble in our direction. Steve calmly stood, shooting at the nearest ones as we all drove through one by one until Shawn stopped the tractor and everyone on board joined in to provide cover for Steve as he pushed the gates closed and climbed back aboard the Volvo. The second his feet hit the seat I pipped my horn to indicate to Shawn it was time to leave.

We picked up speed and retraced our steps back to the church. "It's pretty much one straight road back to the church from here, isn't it?" Chet said as he sat down.

***

I looked in the rear mirror and could see the remaining Zombies following us.

"Yes, mate. There were one or two junctions, but the route is the obvious one to take. Are you thinking what I'm thinking? That in an hour or two, that lot behind will be paying us a visit."

He nodded.

"Let's get back first. There didn't seem to be that many, but you're right, we can't forget about them."

Fifteen minutes and a couple of stray zombies kills later, we arrived back at the church.

With the barricade of cars back in place, we dismounted from the vehicles and began unloading what we'd scavenged.

We were still forty-three and a dog, but we now had an extra vehicle.

CHAPTER SEVEN

With everyone helping, apart from the lookout in the steeple, we soon had the materials unloaded from the vehicles. Stacking it all into similar piles to enable us work out what we had, we began.

Dave had continued weapons training while we'd been gone and when we told him our suspicions that we might soon get more unwelcome visitors, he immediately saw the opportunity to take their training to the next level.

They were ready to start learning patrol skills, and the chance to combine that with some live firing at what we reckoned would only be a small number of the undead, was perfect timing.

He called a quick meeting to decide who was going to do what. He wanted to take one large patrol out consisting of all the new arrivals, with the exception of Bob, the policeman and Dave, the villager we'd first seen in the tower, who both claimed to have some mechanical know-how, making them useful to help in adapting the vehicles. He included a few more 'experienced' ones, just in case.

Gathering nervously together, they listened as Dave and Simon gave them their last few instructions before they left the safety of the churchyard. All holding either an assault rifle or a shotgun with bags containing extra magazines or cartridges over their shoulder, they set off. The knights looked out of place as they held their shields and chosen weapons in their hands, but now with the addition of a modern weapon slung over their shoulders.

Dave told me he'd thought about getting some of them to bring their crossbows, so he could see for himself how effective they would be, but the need for them to gain experience in handling the weapons from this century overrode his curiosity.

Wincing at the noise the generator made when it started, I looked up at the steeple where I could see the children taking their roles as lookouts seriously. They all stood looking through binoculars, ready to warn us at the first sight of anything untoward. The noise we would be making, cutting and drilling, would make us by far the noisiest target in the area and make us a Mecca for any wandering ghouls.

I couldn't dwell on it, though. We had a task to complete and limited time to get it done. I had to trust others to do their jobs. The children had radios with them to communicate with both Simon and Dave, who were leading the patrol, and with us. Dave, ever the planner, had given them a rough plan of the village and instructions on how to read it so they could, via the radios, direct them to any sightings. Most of us in the churchyard had pistols in holsters around our waist and our main guns close to hand to protect the perimeter if need be. All in all, we were in good shape. The churchyard filled with the sound of screeching metal and power tools as we cut, drilled, bolted and welded the framework to the vehicles. It didn't have to be neat, it just needed to be strong enough to do the job and with the experience we'd already gained, progress was swift.

Starting on the bus first, a team constructed the supports for the wedge at the front, while others stripped some seats out from the inside and removed some of the windows to make areas to stand and fight.

One problem we encountered was that we had more jobs to do and people able to use them than power tools available. Work was stopping as people had to wait for others to finish using a certain tool, which was laying idle by their side most of the time when they put it down to fix a bolt or get more material to carry on.

Calling a halt, I reorganised how we worked. One person, who was the most competent in using a particular tool, was allocated it full time. He or she would then go where they were needed and cut or drill or weld for another person and then move on to the next who needed their help. Others I allocated to rotate around the group and help where necessary, either by holding something while bolts were fitted, or by fetching anything needed.

The improvement was immediate and after a bit of shuffling around as people found the role that best suited them, the pace of work really picked up. Soon metal panels, which I was reliably informed were mobile sheep hurdles, were fixed over all the windows, an escape hatch had been cut in the roof and a ladder fixed for access to it. The wedge was taking shape and looked as sturdy, if not more so, than the ones we'd previously constructed.

When what I considered the basics were complete, I moved some teams over to start work on the van. The plan was to complete the bare minimum i.e. the wedge at the front, window protection and an escape hatch to all the vehicles and then, if time and materials permitted, to return to them and do whatever else we could think of to improve them.

The radio clipped to my belt emitted a loud bleeping to indicate someone wanted to talk. The noise we were making made it impossible to hear anything, so I walked to the other side of the church yard.

It was Dave, updating us on their progress.

They'd patrolled the whole village, slowly working their way out from the centre in widening circles, practising drills and manoeuvres as they went along. They had encountered the occasional zombie, usually trapped in a house or car and they'd all had gained real life experience in killing them.

He reported finding plenty of food supplies in most of the houses they'd entered, so that would make it worthwhile planning another trip if time permitted. The idea was worth considering. We had sufficient food now, but there were a lot of us to feed. The plentiful availability of food we had already discussed. The whole country had fallen so quickly to the virus that we knew there should be a lifetime of tinned and preserved foods available from not just households, but supermarkets and the warehouses that supplied them daily. We'd already raided one of the hundreds, if not thousands of lorries transporting all those goods around the country. Finding enough to eat was one of our lesser concerns, but as Shawn had kept repeating his preppers' mantra from the first time we'd met him: 'If it's there, take it.'

If we had the time, and could do it without risk, it was an option worth considering.

They'd found a few pushbikes and he'd send Jim, the Marine, and Noel, the young barman, to scout further afield to see if they could locate the zombies we suspected were heading our way. They had identified a good ambush location on the village outskirts where the road ran between two solid walls, and they were busy training the new recruits on how to reinforce and construct firing positions.

Jim and Noel had been told that if they found them, to lead them to the trap they were busy preparing.

He ended by promising to inform us that they were going to open fire if they appeared, so we wouldn't be alarmed by the sound of guns firing.

The Land Rover with its simple construction and rugged build made it the easiest to convert. Once a few body panels were removed, revealing the chassis, it was a simple job to fix extra supports to it.

I think the boys had got a little more excited about working on the Defender than the other vehicles and the preliminary design that Shawn was working on would turn it into a fully armoured car, completely encased in mesh panels with a mount for a machine gun.

He was struggling with how to design, build and mount a fully rotatable cupola on the roof, though. I attempted to steer the excitable, chatting group as they stood staring at the problem, back onto a more sensible course, but got drawn into the discussion and soon began chipping in with my own ideas.

It took a stern warning from Becky, who had noticed the lack of work going on, to drag us back to the here and now and remind us we still had the basics to complete.

The sound of cutting and drilling and sawing filled the air again. Dave transmitted over the radio that the zombies were in sight, not in numbers to worry about and the firing would begin soon.

The first shots made us stop and listen. The cracks of single rifle shots and the booms of shotguns sounded controlled and not panicked, indicating that Dave and Simon had the situation under control. With complete faith in them, we continued working.

Ten minutes later, Dave reported that they had eliminated them all and were on their way back and reported an ETA of fifteen minutes.

I looked at my watch. It had just passed midday and we had achieved so much already. Okay, we'd been up and about since sunrise at about five am, so we'd already worked a virtual full day, but still, it once again showed what teamwork and cooperation could achieve.

Stanley's excited voice crackled through the radio, telling us that the patrol was in sight.

"Come on, everyone," I said, "Lets open the barricade and welcome them back, I think we deserve a breather for a few minutes."

I turned the generator off and once the ones on patrol had made their weapons safe under the watchful eye of Simon and Dave, and leant them up against the side of the church, they joined us in the shade cast by its high walls, grabbing bottles of water from a few boxes a thoughtful person had got from the church.

As everyone sat, Simon and Dave remained standing and walked into the centre of the circle the group had naturally formed.

"Well done, guys." Simon began, "let's spend a few minutes on an informal after-action report. As far as I'm concerned, you all did great for first timers. You all maintained good gun safety generally."

He looked at the Vicar.

"Even you, Vicar, got the hand of not pointing the dangerous end at anyone eventually."

The vicar smiled and everyone who'd been on the patrol chuckled.

"Thank you, Simon. I forgive you for the profanities you kept shouting at me to remind me, but next time can you keep the good Lord out of it, please?"

"Deal, Vicar. Unless, of course, you decide to point a rifle at me again when I don't not know if it's loaded, or if there's a round in the chamber, or whether the safety might be on or off. Things like that make me forget about being nice. And trust me, Vicar, I was being nice to you earlier."

He waited for the sniggering to subside.

"Anyway. Let's put that aside. You cannot expect to get it right all the time. That's what training is for, so it becomes second nature to you. The bollocking I gave the Vicar was for the benefit of all of you. Trust me, you will all make that mistake and my job is to minimise that and to keep you all safe. He was just the first one I spotted doing it. As for the rest of the patrol: good job. You listened, you never got sloppy and you never hesitated when killing the few we found here and there.

"Marksmanship is something that will come with time. That was the first time most of you have fired a gun and the proof is, you got them all. Neither Dave, nor I or any other of the more experienced shots, fired our weapons in support when they approached. I'm sure you'll be called upon to use your weapons again soon, and the next time you'll find it easier and your accuracy will improve. Overall, well done, now take ten minutes and then go and strip and clean your weapons as we've shown you."

We were still forty-three and a dog, but a more confident forty-three. As for the dog, he was yet to wake up and was lying in the shade of a tree.

CHAPTER EIGHT

Refreshed from the short break, we continued working on the vehicles, determined to get the work done before the end of the day, which would enable us to leave the following morning.

With many more willing hands, the pace of the work picked up even more.

The children were released from lookout duty in the spire and were allowed to run around the churchyard to get rid of their pent-up energy. Horace, the labrador, briefly roused himself to join in with a game of football until apparent exhaustion once again drove him back to the shade of the nearest tree to recover.

Simon spent some time admiring the work that had been done so far to what he was calling 'his' Defender, before sitting down with Shawn and a variety of fittings and clamps we'd scavenged from the farmers' supply shop to try and make a mount for the light machine guns.

By late afternoon we were the proud owners of five heavily armoured zombie-proof vehicles. A few of us were still working on them, because improvements could always be made and as we had so much material available, it seemed a shame not to use it.

The rest of the group, organised by Becky and a few other women, changed focus to loading the vehicles for the journey tomorrow and deciding who would travel in what vehicle.

We reckoned the trailer, with its impregnable high sides, was still the safest transport we had. It was the obvious place for the most precious and vulnerable of the group to travel. Obviously that group was the children, overseen by Maud, and Nicky, who we now knew was pregnant.

The two vehicles that were the easiest to exit from, were the bus and now also, following Shawn's alterations, the trailer. The knights would be split between these two vehicles with the plan forming that they would be the first to 'put feet on the ground', as it were, and protected by their armour and weapons and the rest of us with guns, create a perimeter to enable others to disembark.

The bus looked formidable. It would provide more comfortable transport for a lot of people and still be able to transport a large quantity of supplies. It had a wedge at the front and back and was surrounded by steel sheeting.

We had decided to only fix a wedge to the front of the van. It would carry a portion of our supplies but would have space for more should we find any. Leaving easy access to the rear by not fixing a rear wedge would enable it to be loaded quickly.

Even though the work done to the Land Rover was roughly the same as my Volvo, it just looked a lot cooler. Even though I did try to remain loyal to my trusty Volvo, I did find myself casting an occasional envious glance in its direction.

Shawn and his friends loved it. As preppers, they told us they'd given a lot of thought and discussion time to what would make the best Bug Out Vehicle, or BOV. A Land Rover was always top of their list and they often admired pictures others posted on forum sites showing off their own vehicle.

They assured us that any of our vehicles, but especially the Land Rover, would be the centre of attention at any preppers' convention or meet. The fact that we could now ignore any laws or regulations governing the condition of vehicles allowed on UK roads helped. On a normal day, if we tried to drive any of our vehicles on the roads, we would find ourselves quickly in trouble with the police.

Now the only things trying to stop us would be the undead.

Bob and Dave had yet to go on patrol as they had been helping with the vehicles, so Simon took them out, along with a few others, to give them some experience. Shawn insisted on joining them, saying he hadn't had a chance to try fighting any zombies, wearing his armour yet, and he wanted to get used to the feel of it again.

Much to his friend's amusement, which they tried very badly to hide, Louise helped Shawn on with his armour. He spent time explaining what each piece was called and how it should be buckled and stood there as she reached around him attaching them.

Ian couldn't contain himself anymore and walked over holding an item in his hand. He got her attention and handed it to her.

"Louise, I don't think he had one of these in his kit bag. It's very important that he wears it, we all do when we're fighting."

She looked at what he'd handed her. It was a cricket box. (A shaped plastic cup, edged in padded leather, designed to protect your private parts when batting in cricket). Handing it back, she kept a straight face saying,

"Oh, don't worry, Ian, I've already made sure his is in the right place."

She held it in two fingers and extended her arm to let it dangle in front of Ian's nose.

"Anyway, this must be yours because it's far smaller than the one Shawn has. I can't imagine it'd fit anyone else either, so you may as well have it back."

Completely beaten again and with nowhere to go from such a good put-down, all he could do was accept the dangling box and walk back to his mates, enduring the laughter of them and everyone else who'd heard the exchange.

Simon handed out rucksacks to all who were going on the patrol, explaining that they might as well use the opportunity to gather more supplies. On the previous patrol they'd discovered many full cupboards, therefore the patrol would fulfil two aims: to further everyone's training and to gather extra food that was just sitting there waiting to be scavenged.

The lookout in the Spire reported seeing a few more zombies approaching. We were the noisiest thing around and as long as we remained so, they would always be attracted to us.

Once they were ready, the patrol, after a last equipment check and briefing reminding them about the need for safety and to be constantly alert, scrambled over the church wall and walked across the village green in the direction the zombies were reported to be approaching from.

Soon, the occasional flurry of shots reminded us that danger was never far away.

By the time they returned an hour later, each carrying a bulging rucksack, the vehicles were all loaded, and their contents secured against shifting during the journey. We were ready to go as soon as dawn broke the following morning.

Simon and Dave organised a whole community drill, so people would know what to expect when on the road.

Everyone boarded their allocated vehicles and once the vehicles were full of passengers, it became obvious that some of the contents would need to be shifted around. We practised a few scenarios until we were satisfied we had the best configuration of people and supplies.

We then had everyone practise using the spears and hand weapons to fight imaginary zombies surrounding the vehicles.

This highlighted a few minor improvements that would make it easier for the ones on the bus to fight.

The knights then trained on exiting the trailer and bus as effectively as possible.

The bus proved simple. Holding their shields ready, once the door was opened and the metal gate reinforcing them swung back on its hinges, they could exit the bus two at a time and create a shield wall, holding back any threats as more exited from behind to support them. After a few attempts and changes to the tactics, they'd worked out the best way to do it.

The procedure to exit the trailer, on the other hand, needed more work and thought to get it right.

The rear door swung open easily enough and the ramp could be deployed with not much effort. It was when they walked down the ramp, potential problems became obvious. The angle and narrowness of the ramp made walking down it difficult, especially when encumbered with the full weight of their armour. It was hard to swing their weapons or protect each other with their shields until they reached the ground, which meant the first few down would be vulnerable.

When they were clear of the ramp, they could form their defensive wall and fight effectively. With practice this could be done reasonably quickly, and the ramp raised, and trailer door shut, protecting the occupants inside. If the ramp was made wider, it would become too heavy to move quickly and potentially expose the ones left in the trailer to danger.

No easy solution came to mind, apart from not exiting the vehicle at all when there were too many zombies. So we decided to adhere to that policy.

Anyway, from experience, we thought we probably had enough firepower to keep any at bay, without the need to step down from the vehicles and we could always keep moving to find a safer place to stop, if need be.

The light machine guns were mounted on brackets Simon and Shawn had devised for the trailer and much to my jealousy, also for his Land Rover.

It now looked even better.

From their fixed positions, they could lay down an accurate and deadly amount of firepower. The Marines assured us that they alone should be enough to keep us safe, without even considering all the other weapons we had.

The bulk of the work was done, and finding myself as a loose end, I went to find Becky. I wanted to spend some time together, even if it was only a few moments.

Taking her hand, we walked away from the others and sat on a bench in the shade of a tree.

We were far enough away to get some privacy, but still able to view most of the churchyard and all the activity still going on.

The children had stopped running around and were all sitting together under the shade of another tree, laughing and talking as if they didn't have a care in the world.

Laying our weapons aside, but still within easy reach, I held out my arm and she leant against my chest and we silently hugged for a few minutes, both just taking in what was going on around us.

"This all still seems so unreal," Becky said quietly, "Occasionally I've found myself thinking that this is all a dream and soon I'll wake up in our caravan at St Agnes and we'll head off to the beach again. But that life, normal life, now seems so far away and distant that it can't be a dream. What we've done and experienced over…" She stopped and thought for a while.

"How long has it been now, Tom? A week now? I can't even remember. It's unbelievable, but what we're doing now seems normal. Two weeks ago, I was pushing a shopping trolley around a supermarket, rushing so I could make it to the gym class before picking up the kids from school. And now, I'm sitting on a bench in a churchyard watching over my kids, ready to grab a gun and without hesitation shoot in the head what was once a normal person, just like you and me, just so my children can live to see another day. Tell me I'm dreaming, Tom, please.

"I used to get annoyed at other Moms on the school run and their pathetic attempts to drive their stupidly big cars, wishing sometimes I had a gun so I could wreak my revenge. And now, you know what? I have a gun and would probably, without a second thought, use it on them, just because they deserve it. Is that wrong?"

I chuckled.

"And you used to moan at me and my road rage. Just be thankful that school runs are a thing of the past, so you won't have to."

She snuggled in closer.

"I don't think you could write this story. Look at what we've done, who we've met and what we've achieved. It just doesn't seem believable. If you hadn't got us out of that campsite, and at the time I went along with it even I thought you were having some sort of breakdown, we would be dead along with millions of others. You knew what to do."

She was quiet for a few minutes.

"I haven't said thank you yet. Thank you, Tom, for saving us. I now think we stand a chance to survive and make whatever life we can out of all the chaos that's happened."

A few more minutes of silence and quiet understanding passed between us.

I looked across the churchyard and all the activity still going on.

Geoff, Alex and Jamie were holding crossbow instruction for anyone who wanted a go, using a large oak tree as a target. The value of those weapons hadn't been fully explored, with everything else going on. I'd fought beside Shawn as he'd used his when we thought we were done for at the farm on the moors and it seemed like an age ago now. Up to a certain range, the crossbows were effective and silent killers and all his friends had brought a few each with them and a large supply of bolts, so there were a lot to go around.

Shawn and Jim were still tinkering with the vehicles, all the time adding to the strength and effectiveness of them.

Shane and Steve the Marine had now taken Stanley, Eddie and Jim, and Bob's children Charlie, Bertie and Josh and Victoria's son, also called Josh, to the church wall and had begun to teach them how to use the .22 rimfire rifles.

While they'd slept last night, we'd agreed it would be a good idea to start their training as soon as possible. The .22 rimfire rifles were amongst the rifles we'd collected from Shane's gun shop and with their low recoil, they were a great introductory gun to train them on, and a proven zombie killer after using the one I'd got from the farm to great effect. Before I had 'upgraded' to a more powerful military grade weapon.

Shane and Steve had volunteered to instruct them. The other parents and I agreed that having a non-family member and relative stranger teaching them would be a good idea and make them concentrate more.

I watched, and they were all listening intently and being as grown up as possible. Not one of them wanted the warnings given to come true, and not be allowed to fire them if they messed about and couldn't be trusted.

"Becky, darling. I know there's nothing we can do about it, but do we need to worry about the children? Most of them have already killed their fair share of zombies with the spears and all of them have witnessed sights that wouldn't be allowed in most horror movies. It must be having a deep and profound effect on all of us, so what will it be doing to the children? They're killers now. The rules of the world have changed. It's now acceptable to kill. I'm sure a psychologist will have long and fancy words for it, but I just don't want it to fuck them up, that's all. One day some sort of normality may return, and they'll need to be able to adjust."

We both watched as the children, under close supervision, began to fire the guns, aiming at the various cars lying abandoned around the village green. Their excitement at hitting something they were aiming at was evident from where we sat.

The skills they were being taught were not for shooting for fun at targets or tin cans, the things children would usually practise with when first learning to shoot. But rather to end the existence of something that had once lived, but which now wanted to attack any of us to satisfy its hunger for human flesh; and all to keep the virus alive and spreading.

"Well, Tom," Becky said with a sigh, "all we can do is keep a close eye on them and keep giving them the chance, when we can, to just be children. To run around and play and forget the world around them.

And when do you really think this will be over? We need to reach this castle we're all hoping will provide the sanctuary it promises, and then take it from there. We don't know how long those things will keep going. Will they rot and fall apart eventually, or will they go on forever? There are millions out there all over the country. We can't kill them all, just the ones that are threatening us. We could be stuck behind the walls of Warwick Castle for a long time."

"Who knows is the answer to that. All we can do is take each day as it comes and keep going. If all goes well, we might even reach Warwick tomorrow, but I doubt it. We've got to try and find Louise's family near Cheltenham and then Steve's in Worcester first, and who knows how long that will take? We'll plan the route and all the alternatives tonight, but I imagine it'll be slow going. Five vehicles won't travel as fast as two, and we're restricted by the speed the tractor can go. Two days at best is my guess."

I looked at the vehicles. Shawn and Jim were still working on them, using the time to add more fixings or extra bits on here and there. They looked great. Yes, they were not as neat as they could have been if they'd had the benefit of a machine shop and all the specialist equipment it contained. What we'd previously done had been tried and tested and was known to work. Using that experience, they knew what was needed and given the limited time and proper materials, they'd worked wonders.

They would all protect the occupants and each vehicle would have its own use. The bus and the van would transport most of our equipment and people. The tractor with its weight and power should be able to clear blockages and cleave through zombies. The trailer it towed provided an impregnable fortress and an excellent fighting platform. The Volvo and Land Rover, both heavily protected and modified, could go wherever they were needed; to scout ahead or be agile enough to thin out the undead and provide protection and support for the other vehicles.

A lot of the materials we had got from the farmers' supplies shop remained unused. We decided to reload the most useful items onto the trailer we'd already got, and hitch it up again to Simon's Defender. If we got into any trouble or needed it, it could easily be unhitched and left behind or reattached after we'd finished whatever we were doing.

We had the radios to communicate with each other to coordinate on the move. Shawn had already said he would keep a lookout for vehicles with citizen band (CB) radios fitted, as they would make communication easier and extend the range. Even with the advent of mobile phones making them obsolete, he knew some truckers still preferred to use them, so he was confident that given time he would find enough for us all.

We both stood up to join the others, refreshed by the normality of having the chance to sit down and spend time together.

Everyone else was also finishing their various tasks. The final items were being loaded onto the vehicles, and the children were finishing off cleaning the guns they'd been using. One by one as jobs were completed, the group slowly drifted into church, attracted by the delicious smells of cooking food wafting out of the door.

Forty-three people and a dog that had now woken up and looked hungry gathered in the church for their last night.

CHAPTER NINE

We waited patiently in our vehicles as the Vicar bustled around, carrying the last few items he wanted to save from the church to the bus. There were no items of real value, but he told us that that if he was going to continue to look after our spiritual wellbeing, he needed the tools of his trade with him.

Once the last vehicle had left the churchyard, we pushed the barrier back into place and made sure everything was secure. As with the farm on the moors, it had provided us with safe shelter and it would for any others that might come across it if we left it secured. A sign was nailed to the door explaining who we were, where we had come from and where we eventually intended to reach.

We left a small cache of supplies as a gift.

Forming the convoy, everyone stood at their allocated positions and watched as the church fell from view.

Dave, following the map and the route we had marked on it with his finger, gave me advanced warning of approaching turns. The plan was to head to the M5 motorway, which we knew was clear after meeting the soldiers who had come from Cheltenham, and making the best speed we could, then to leave the motorway at the nearest exit to the small village where Louise's parents lived.

Maintaining a slow but steady speed, we drove down narrow country lanes. I couldn't see much from my position at the rear of the convoy, only seeing the evidence from the warnings given over the radio of a vehicle pushed to one side to clear the way, or zombies crushed by one of the vehicles in front or re-killed by a spear as they passed them.

By the time ones that had fallen victim to the plough emerged from underneath the vehicle in front of me, there was not much left of them. The occasional one would still be thrashing about, even though most of it had been mangled beyond recognition, showing that unless you destroyed the brain, they could still be a threat. I always tried to aim for the head to end another one's existence.

An hour later and not encountering anything that gave us a problem, we drove down the slip road and onto the motorway. The way ahead, as we had been promised, was clear and Shawn picked up the speed. Steering around abandoned vehicles, the miles slipped away.

Louise's voice came over the radio, stopping our chatter. "Slowing down. There is something written on the side of a van ahead."

Slowing to a crawl, we followed in a line until a call over the radio told us to stop.

I pulled out from behind the van to see what was going on.

A van was sitting across two lanes of the motorway. Writing was crudely sprayed in large red letters along its side.

'ROAD CLOSED. PAY A TRIBUTE TO PASS'

"What the hell?" I said, "The soldiers didn't tell us about this."

Dave was looking ahead through some binoculars.

"It may not have been here a few days ago. I can't see much from down here."

He picked up the radio and asked if anyone could see what was going on ahead.

Shawn came back.

"The road looks to be completely blocked about a mile ahead, but I can't make out much more than that. We need to get closer."

Simon pulled up beside me and stood on his seat. I did the same, so we could all talk.

"Dave. It's time to see if the scout vehicle theory works. Both of us will go and check it out. Leave everyone else here, there's enough of them to protect themselves.

These guys, whoever they are, are not military. Who asks for a tribute these days? It's probably some punks hoping to score some easy supplies from some poor sod."

"What happens if they're a group like us?" Chet asked from the seat behind me. "Do we give them something to let us through?"

Dave turned to him.

"I can guarantee they will not be like us. That sign says it all. I can't tell you how many similar signs I've seen in pisspot countries all over the world. It will be some local wanna be hard knocks thinking they can get easy pickings without having to work for it. The problem is in most third world countries, those kids carry AK47s so you have to handle it carefully. Here, we haven't a clue what, if at all, they'll be armed with. We should do this carefully and let me do the talking."

"Simon, unhook the trailer and stay to our side to cover us with the gun. Everyone else, get your weapons up and ready. We may as well show them we aren't to be messed with."

I looked up at Becky, who was looking at me from the side of the trailer. Stanley and Daisy stood by her side, and they all had worried looks on their faces.

I waved and mouthed 'I love you' at them, then I slid down in my seat and started the car and pulled slowly forward.

Simon followed slightly behind me and to the side. Jim stood ready, standing on the passenger seat of the Defender, his shoulder pressed against the mounted machine gun, ready to fire if necessary.

Dave, Chet and Daniel stood on the seats, all holding a weapon visible and ready.

The closer we got, the clearer it was to make out that the motorway was completely blocked by a barricade of cars and vans. I couldn't see beyond that from my position in the driving seat, but from Dave's vantage point standing up, he reported that it looked as if they'd had formed a small fort of cars surrounding a few lorries. Its position by a bridge going over the motorway would make it impossible to get around.

I saw a few heads looking over the cars facing us as we drew closer.

Dave had the binoculars pressed to his eyes.

"I can see a few of them, can't make out how many there are, but it does look as if they have some guns with them."

He chuckled, "Well, with my eyesight they're either broomsticks or guns, but they're holding them as if they're guns, so that'll do. Let's assume they're armed and not particularly friendly. It can only get better from that position."

I stopped about fifty metres away.

A man stood up on the barricade. He held a rifle with the stock pressed against his hip and the barrel pointing up into the air.

Dave muttered, "Look at the idiot. Does he think he's fucking Rambo or something? The only thing holding a rifle that way will impress is his own ego."

The man shouted something, but the distance made it unintelligible.

"Pull closer," said Dave. "When we stop, keep it in reverse and be ready to go if I shout." And to everyone else. "If you see anyone point a gun in our direction, do not hesitate, shoot them. I do not have a good feeling about this."

Three cars lay abandoned ahead, doors open, their contents scattered around them.

"I'd say from the look of those cars, these boys have met a few others," Dave muttered quietly.

Passing the cars, I could see a few bloodstains, but no evidence of bodies.

Dave signalled me to stop twenty metres from the wall of cars.

He shouted in a friendly manner. "Hello. How are you doing? You seem to have a nice set-up here and we would love to stop and chat, but we need to continue our journey. If you would kindly move some cars out of the way, we will be past and on our way before you know it."

The man, who was still standing on the bonnet of a car and holding what looked to be a hunting rifle, stared back at us.

He was in his early twenties and was wearing jeans and despite the heat, a leather jacket. I think he was taken aback by the intimidating sight of our vehicles, with men standing, some in uniform pointing not just assault rifles and shotguns at him, but a machine gun mounted on the Land Rover.

He turned and spoke to others hidden behind the barricade, more heads slowly appearing. I couldn't see any more firearms, but that didn't mean they didn't have them just out of sight.

He seemed more confident now he had more support.

"Did you not see the sign? We own this piece of road now and in return for us keeping it clear of walkers, you must pay to pass. What do you have to pay us with? If you're from the Army, then as we're doing your job, you must give us some of your guns so we can keep helping people."

I heard a few snorts of laughter from behind the barricade.

"I am not authorised to give weapons to non-military people, son, so that's not going to happen."

Dave waved his arm at the cars lying abandoned around us, with their contents haphazardly dumped all around them.

"And if you're helping people as you say, what happened to the ones in these cars?"

"They, er… didn't want our help and decided to walk from here," he said, a smile spreading across his face.

Dave stared at him long and hard.

"Son, are you going to let us through? I haven't got the time or patience to get into a pissing competition with you. You will not get any guns from us, full stop. But if you let us through, we can give you some other stuff that might be of use to you."

The man, obviously feeling he had the upper hand, despite all the guns pointing at him, replied.

"No guns, no pass."

Dave sat down next to me.

"He must be off his head on drugs or something if he can't see the danger that he's facing. But the problem is, we don't know what we're facing either, and I'm not going to risk getting into a needless fight with those idiots. I'm sure we'd win easily, but one of us might get injured or worse. They're just not worth it. They're up to no good and any other day I would say we deal with them, but we need to keep moving and not put any of us at risk. I say we turn around and find another route. Just let me check with Simon to see if he agrees."

He picked up the radio and explained his feelings to Simon. He also agreed that even though he wanted to teach the young idiot a lesson in manners and humanity using his knuckles, caution would be the best policy.

Dave stood up on his seat again.

"Okay, you win. We'll find another way. Before we go, though. You may think you're big and hard hiding behind those cars, stealing off whatever poor sods you find. But haven't you noticed the world has gone to shit and whatever game you think you're playing will only end badly for you unless everyone starts helping each other."

The man laughed at him.

"Piss off, old man. We can do what we want, and no one can stop us…"

I couldn't hear the rest of his words as I reversed the car and turned it around.

Dave, who had heard the rest of what he'd said, was fuming.

He wanted to jump from the car and beat the crap out of him.

I was trying to calm him down when Daniel, who was still standing on the seat behind me, facing towards the road block as we drove away from it, was thrown backwards, followed immediately by the loud BOOM of a gun being fired.

His limp body slumped down, and he came to a rest facing upwards at an angle between the front seats with his head resting on my lap. His face was a bloody mess. Blood poured from the back of his head, covering me.

I screamed in shock and panic. He had obviously been shot and was in a bad way. I slammed my foot on the brakes of the car, so I could tend to him.

Dave roared at me.

"Fucking drive!" And then to everyone else, "Fire! They're shooting at us."

With one hand on Daniel's ruined head, I put my foot down hard on the accelerator. As the car shot forwards, I was deafened by Dave and Chet firing their weapons at the receding barricade. I could hear the machine gun firing controlled bursts from the Land Rover as it too sped along beside me.

Futilely stroking his head, I was shouting over and over, "Daniel, you're going to be okay. Hang on in there," as the car sped towards the rest of our convoy.

I was soaked in his blood. I glanced at him, knowing but not wanting to accept, than no one could survive the devasting wound he had received.

Ahead I could see the tractor, bus and van already turning around. They could see and hear we were in trouble and were heading back at breakneck speed, so they'd had the presence of mind to start moving.

I slowed down as I neared the convoy, staying behind them as we drove down the motorway, back the way we had come. Chet was still firing long bursts, but Dave stopped and leant down into the vehicle.

He took one look at Daniel and screamed.

"Fucking bastards." He quickly sat back on the seat and reaching into a pouch, pulled out an aid kit. He raised his head, inspecting the wound and held a wound dressing against the back of his head. Placing his head gently back he said quietly,

"I think he's gone, mate."

Tears flowed down my cheeks and I kept stroking his head, not wanting to accept the truth.

Soon Simon's voice came over the radio.

"We are out of sight of them. Let's stop and regroup."

Chet had also stopped firing when he looked down at Daniel as he lay sprawled across the car. Chet now sat in the rear seat, silently staring at Daniel, tears flowing down his cheeks.

In a dream-like state from the shock, I stopped when the others did.

Chet and I were out of it, unable to process what had happened in the last sixty seconds. Dave took control.

"Simon. We have a man down. Daniel's been shot. You maintain the perimeter while I deal with it."

I didn't hear the rest of the exchange but was aware of Dave jumping out of the vehicle. Moments later, he jumped back up and standing on the bonnet of the car, he leant through the hole on the roof.

"Tom."

I ignored him.

He gently tapped me on the shoulder.

"Come on, Tom. We need to get him out of there, so I can check him properly."

That snapped me out of wherever I was. "Of course. How shall we do this?"

"Lift him up and I'll get his shoulders. Chet, support his head and hold that dressing on as we lift him."

Chet leant forward, his hands quickly covering in blood as he held Daniel's head in both hands. I reached under his arms, struggling to lift the dead weight as Dave reached down to help. Chet's arms were fully extended and he couldn't hold the bandage in place any longer and it fell back into the car. More blood poured over me as we struggled. It became easier when Chet lifted his legs, so he wasn't tangled between the seats.

With one final unceremonious heave, Dave pulled him out through the roof and called for help. Within seconds, more helpers appeared, and he was quickly lifted from the car and he disappeared from my view as he was laid on the ground.

I sat staring at the blood on my hands and clothes.

Becky calling my name roused me once again and I stood on the seat and climbed out of the Volvo. As soon as she saw me, she screamed.

"Oh, my God, Tom! Are you hurt?"

I was coated in blood. My clothes, my hands and my face were all covered.

"No, no, Darling. It's not mine. It's Daniel's. They shot him as we were driving away."

All eyes were on the few attending to Daniel. All crouching around his prone body. Two minutes of fervent activity later they all slowly stood as one and stared at his body. Dave walked away from the group, returning with a blanket which he laid over it.

The act, a clear signal to us all, that we had lost one of our own.

I stood staring at his corpse, the anger welling up inside me. We had all witnessed people dying since this began, but they had been killed by the undead. Screaming and fighting as they were overwhelmed, howling in pain as the first bites and gouges were taken from their living flesh.

Daniel had not died that way. He had been killed by a fellow survivor and that did not seem right. As a group, all *we* had done was help other survivors when we met them.

The harsh reality of the new world we lived in slammed home. It wasn't just the walking dead we needed to protect ourselves from. Evil wasn't just confined to them. Evil was still rife amongst the living. At a time when humanity needed to band together, to help each other to survive to see another dawn, there were some who did not see the world that way.

The group each showed their grief in their own way, we all had tears running down our faces, but some stood sobbing, baring their raw emotions to the world while others stood silently, grim faces betraying the rage and anger they felt.

Forty-two people and one dog stood in the sunshine on the M5 motorway. The blanket covered corpse of one of the group marked another day we would never forget.

CHAPTER TEN

Needing to reorganise, and with no zombies in sight, we pulled the vehicles into a protective ring. Shawn backed the tractor to fill the final gap and the rear door of the trailer swung open, the ramp lowered to allow those inside to disembark. Simon told a few to stay on guard while the rest of us gathered within the protection the vehicles provided.

Geoff, wearing his armour and his mace resting on his shoulders, walked up to Dave.

"What are we going to do about those bastards? We can't let them get away with this."

"Fifteen minutes ago," Dave began. "I was suggesting we find another way round them. It wasn't worth risking any of us to try and fight through them.

Now though, I personally want to go and kill every last one of them to make them pay for what they've done. They cannot continue doing to others what they've done to us. I feel we have a duty to anyone who is still surviving out there to deal with them."

He paused and looked around.

"But this needs to be a group decision. We still have a mission to complete and any delays could have consequences for those family members and friends we're going to try to find."

All eyes turned to Louise and Steve. They were the ones whose families we had promised to get to, and therefore, could directly be affected by any delays caused in getting to them.

Louise spoke first. Shawn was standing beside her and she took his hand, and wiping away the tears from her face, she spoke confidently.

"I don't know if any of my family are still alive. I hope to God they are, but in reality, I think we all know that the chances of finding them living are very remote. I do want to try, though, because not knowing would be worse. If they're gone, then I can deal with that, but a part of me knows that they most probably are, and is already grieving for them.

Daniel was one of us. Part of our new family, if you want to put it that way. His death cannot go unanswered and as Dave quite rightly said, they cannot be allowed to continue. We owe it to everyone still living to eradicate anyone we come across who thinks they can use the new shitty world we're living in to cause suffering and death to others."

I think we were all impressed by the eloquence and passion of her speech and we all remained silent for a few moments, digesting her words.

Steve spoke next. He put it more simply.

"Daniel was a great bloke. Those bastards need to pay for what they've done. I say we go get 'em."

I looked around, catching the eye of each one of them as they all silently nodded their agreement. The game had changed. Not only were zombies our targets, but survivors. Albeit ones that that had lost their humanity.

The planning began.

Simon and Dave spread a map out. The nearest exit from the motorway was about five miles behind us. Tracing the route back from the bridge that crossed the motorway above where the gang had constructed their camp, we could see the road did lead to that junction.

A frontal assault was briefly discussed. We could lay down an overwhelming amount of fire, but we didn't know how many guns we'd be facing, and they'd already proved that at least one of them was a good, or maybe just a lucky, shot. That was deemed too risky.

The map showed that the road leading to the bridge ran parallel to where we were, and it was only a few hundred yards away across the fields adjacent to our current position.

Dave sent a small patrol out to investigate if the road could be accessed from the motorway. They returned, reporting that apart from the wooden fence that kept livestock from wandering on to the carriageway, the gates in the fields enabled access to the road.

When questioned further, they reckoned that not only the Volvo and the Land Rover would easily make it, but the van should too. The fields, baked by the long hot spell we were experiencing, sloped gently enough so it shouldn't lose traction or get bogged down.

Gathering everyone around, Dave explained the plan.

I would take the lead in the Volvo and the van would follow me, breaking through the fence and making our way across the fields until we joined the road.

All the Marines would be included in the mission, supported by half of the knights and five others. They would pack into my car and the van.

The Land Rover would approach to within effective range of the barricade and open fire. This would hopefully get their attention and keep their heads down. Shane, who had proved to be a crack shot, would either fire at any target that presented itself from the Land Rover or disembark from it if a better position could be found. A knight would accompany him for protection from zombies.

Once we got close enough to the bridge, we would approach on foot. The knights would provide the protection, killing any zombies silently with their weapons to enable us to get into position without drawing attention to ourselves.

Dave and Simon would then reconnoitre forward to plan the final attack. A radio call telling everyone to cease fire, once acknowledged, would signal the start of the assault.

Everyone else would remain behind, sealed up in the tractor, trailer and bus. There was enough of them to defend both and if need be, they could start up and use their ploughs to destroy the undead if they became too numerous.

A simple plan, but one that needed separate groups to coordinate. Dave and Simon both expressed a high confidence in our abilities and in a successful outcome.

Once again, time would tell.

Fifteen minutes later, the buzzing of this hive of activity had come to an end. All were in their allocated positions. Weapons and ammo had been checked and double checked. The ones chosen to man the machine guns, both in the Land Rover and trailer, had received a crash course in how to fire and reload them from Jim and Simon.

Following agreement from the parents, the children who had begun their training on using the .22 rimfire rifles the day before were issued with them. All of the trained Marines and a good portion of the more experienced 'civilians' were going on the mission. Therefore, the addition of another five armed people in the trailer would offer extra security, and peace of mind for those of us not going to be there.

After a final wave at loved ones and friends, we prepared to leave. The Land Rover drove slowly forward and disappeared from view over the crest of the road. Soon the harsh sound of the machine gun fire shattering the silence signalled it was our time to depart.

The van followed closely as I drove up the grassy bank that lined the motorway. Slowing as I approached the wooden fence, I aimed at the middle point between posts and kept going. The rails cracked and broke, the simple act of destroying something making me smile as we bumped across the fields, heading towards a gate in the corner. Finding none of the gates locked, we were soon on the road heading for the bridge. Driving slowly to keep the noise down, we crept towards the spot we'd picked out on the map as the best place to leave the vehicles to approach the final distance on foot, and we disembarked, standing in a group around Dave and Simon, waiting for our final instructions. Dave spoke quietly.

"Right then, guys and gals. Simon and I will check the lie of the land ahead."

He pointed at Jamie who was wearing his full armour and had his axe over his shoulder.

"Could you come with us, please, to watch our backs and to deal with any undead? The rest of you wait here. I don't need to tell you to stay alert. The amount of noise we have been and still are making will surely be attracting them from miles around. To be fair, I'm surprised none have appeared yet.

Jim, you're in charge while we're gone, so the rest of you, just do whatever he bloody tells you. Okay?"

Without further ado, he turned and with Jamie following, his armour clinking at every step, and Simon bringing up the rear, they set off down the road and disappeared around a bend.

Following Jim's instructions, the rest of us who remained crouched in an outward facing circle. The only sound was the not-too-distant rattle of the machine gun interspersed with spaced single cracks from what must have been Shane sniping at any targets of opportunity.

I crouched, holding my rifle in the ready position as I had been shown, my trigger finger lying flat against the weapon, just above the trigger, ready for anything that might come towards us. I felt tense and glancing around, I was sure the others felt the same. We'd fought zombies dozens of times already, mainly from the relative safety of the vehicles, or on foot only when it was completely unavoidable, or when the odds were in our favour. This was the largest operation we had mounted, and it was against the living.

I didn't feel any moral objections to what we were about to do. They had needlessly killed one of us and had, no doubt, in their hopefully short reign of terror, killed others or condemned them to die by stealing whatever possessions they had and refusing to offer shelter. At no other time in human history had mankind needed to work together, to forget differences, be they political, race, gender or whatever, to survive.

But despite all that, the bad side of human nature could override basic common decency. It didn't take a genius to work out that there would be enough supplies and equipment lying abandoned in shops, warehouses and homes to keep the surviving population going for a long time. This was due to how quickly the virus had spread, but you just had to be brave enough and organised enough to go and get it.

Some, though, would still take the easy option and steal from others. These were the first of such scum we had come across and I was certain they wouldn't be the last. How we dealt with others we found needed to be discussed between us when the time was right.

The sound of chinking armour drew my attention in the direction Simon, Jamie and Dave had left.

They rounded the bend at a full sprint, Jamie, even though he was carrying a full weight of armour, keeping up with them.

Breathing heavily from the exertion, Dave spoke.

"The situation has changed. There's a massive horde heading down the motorway towards their position. I can't tell how many, but they stretch back as far as I can see. There must be thousands of them. All I know is that it's bigger than the one we faced back at the base. I don't think their walls will keep them safe, there are just too many of them. Not that I care what happens to them. My concern is that they're heading towards us."

He looked at us.

"Anybody have any suggestions?"

My first thought was to get back to my family. If the horde was as big as Dave was telling us, we needed all of us together to protect ourselves.

"I vote we go back now. Their defences won't hold against that many, so they're done for. Let's get the zombies to do our dirty work for us."

Most nodded in agreement and started back towards the vehicles.

Dave, the knight, stopped us.

"Hang on, folks. Why don't we help the zombies out a bit? We came here to kill those bastards. If we can knock a few holes in their walls and stop them escaping over the others, job done."

Dave, the Marine, answered.

"So, you're suggesting we use the zombies as a weapon?"

"Yes, mate. They did it a few times on the *Walking Dead*."

"Are you are suggesting we adopt tactics from a made-up TV show?"

He laughed, "It's not so made up now, is it? I do think we should watch the show again as a sort of training video. We're living in the same world now, and most of what happened to them might happen to us. It should give us some good ideas."

It was Dave's turn to laugh.

"Right, then. All of my years of military experience are being overridden by some script writer in America? Oh well. I can't think of anything better, so let's get on with it. If we put our foot down, we're less than ten minutes away from the others, so we've got plenty of time to do this and get back. Are we all in agreement?"

We all were, our anger at Daniel's death fuelling our need for revenge.

"Simon, get on the radio and let everyone know what's going on. Tell whoever is on the machine gun to stop firing. We don't want any stray rounds coming our way, but tell Shane to continue sniping. From what I saw, they've already got a few of them and it'll keep them concentrating in our direction watching us and not watching the way the zombies are coming from…"

"Watch out!"

Two zombies had approached unnoticed and appeared from around the side of the van, ten metres from where we were all gathered.

We all raised our weapons and took aim. Simon quickly shouted.

"Don't fire, we need to keep quiet."

***

"Don't worry, we've got this," Jamie cheerfully replied. "Geoff, with me, mate. I'll take the one on the left."

They both casually sauntered up to the pair. One looked to be untouched by any injuries so most likely succumbed in the initial stages of the virus spreading. His clothes were ripped and tattered, probably from his wanderings as an undead monster looking for his next meal. The other was a woman who was naked, her wounds visible for us all to see. Her neck had an obvious bite wound and her stomach had been ripped open so her intestines bulged out, hampering her progress as she kept stumbling on a trailing piece of gut.

Had they been husband and wife? Had the man turned first and attacked his wife as she slept beside him, infecting and turning her? The bonds of their relationship seemed to be somehow keeping them together in their new existence.

Jamie swung his axe, taking the woman's head clean off her shoulders. Geoff swung his mace overhead next, the man's head caved in and brains and blood sprayed out of his ears, nose and mouth.

I watched as they fell, their bodies falling on each other, the man's arms lying across what might have been his loved one in a final embrace.

Simon got our attention.

"I'll take the blame for that. Bloody rooky mistake, though. We stopped checking our perimeter when we were all having a lovely chat."

He looked at Dave.

"Maybe we do need to watch the Walking Dead. I need to get up to speed on this zombie thing. Right then, let's get on with this."

He took a radio out of his pocket and informed the others what we were planning to do and to get ready for our speedy return.

Once they had all acknowledged, we got ready.

The machine gun falling silent was our signal to approach the bridge, seeking shelter under some trees that would hide us, but give us a view of our target, and once in situ, we planned what to do next.

The horde of approaching zombies was clearly visible. They filled the motorway from side to side, hemmed in by the fences, and stretched back as far as I could see, easily numbering in their thousands, maybe tens of thousands.

It looked as if the entire undead population of a town or city had left as one mass, searching for their next meal.

I remembered watching a documentary a while before about migrating animals, and it said that sometimes the herds grew so massive that the ones at the back starved to death due to the lead ones eating all the available food as they cut a swathe through the land on their journey to fresh grazing. The similarity was eerie, but probably true.

All the available food sources in an area i.e. humans, had been exhausted where they were and now they'd gathered together and, as one, had started to move on to find a new source.

They were migrating, forming a massive and unstoppable tide of undead flesh-eating monsters. We'd already observed and agreed that they tended to coalesce, some primeval programming still left in the brain probably telling them that they could hunt better together in packs.

Would these individual groups eventually meet and form a super herd? Probably, I guessed.

We could, one day, find ourselves facing millions of them.

Our objective, Warwick Castle, needed to be reached as soon as possible. We didn't yet know if it would be suitable. If it was, I imagined there would be a lot of work do to make it impregnable against an untold number. Time was of the essence and if it ran out and we weren't fully ready, we could be in serious trouble with nowhere left to run.

The thugs hadn't spotted them yet and were all, as far as we could tell, crouching behind the bullet-scarred barricade, facing the direction where the firing was coming from. Occasionally one of them fired a wildly aimed shot in that general direction. Not all of them were armed, but most did have either a shotgun or rifle. We were in a rural area, so one or more of them had either owned them or known where to get them from.

I counted four bodies lying amongst them, victims of either Shane or the machine gun.

Simon began positioning us amongst the trees, picking spots where we could each fire upon them if need be. He, Dave and the other two Marines then ran in a low crouch onto the bridge, staying in the middle to avoid being spotted, and crawled to positions directly overlooking their site.

The horde kept coming, each shambling step bringing them closer, their groans and sounds of thousands of bodies stumbling along audible to us now between the crack of Shane's high-powered rifle. It would only be a matter of time before our enemies heard them too.

Glancing around, I could see we all had our weapons raised, everyone using a tree or fallen branch as cover, silently observing them through their sights. Dave, Jamie and Geoff, holding their weapons, faced the other way, ready to protect us from any that might appear from the other direction.

One of the gang eventually became aware of the noises coming from the direction opposite that which they were facing. Curiosity made him brave, despite the sporadic incoming fire, and he ran towards the opposite barricade. Standing still for a few seconds, he stared, gawping at the approaching, terrifying spectacle. His brain slowly comprehended what he was looking at and he cupped his hands to his mouth to shout a warning.

A single shot rang out from one of the Marines on the bridge and he fell before he could raise the alarm. This shot, being fired from a new, close and unknown location caused immediate panic amongst the remaining gang members, who crouching even lower, urgently looked around to try and identify the new threat. A few shots were fired, but nothing came anywhere near us.

Their fallen comrade lay unnoticed at the other barricade, the blood from the single gunshot to his chest staining the road around him.

The throng of zombies, stretching back along the motorway was almost up to the wall of vehicles. We had been warned what the Marines planned to do, so when Dave bellowed, "Cover!" everyone threw themselves down flat behind whatever cover they were already behind.

The four metal orbs, thrown by experienced arms and aimed at the same spot, exploded simultaneously. The shockwave from the exploding grenades passed over us and we looked up. A hole had been blown in the barricade, one of the cars lay on its roof, burning, and the smoke and dust cloud blanketed the area, making it hard to see beyond that spectacle.

Knocked off their feet by the explosion, the gang members slowly picked themselves up and stared at the hole that had inexplicably been blown in their defences.

Panic replaced their stunned silence when the first zombies appeared, staggering through the wall of smoke and dust. Not having the ability to know or care, some had walked through the flames pouring from the car and had caught fire themselves, their fiercely burning clothes turning them into human torches.

Unable to feel pain, they carried on walking, heading towards the now completely panicking and freaking out gang members.

Those with some presence of mind held their ground, raised their weapons and fired. The zombies pressed by the uncountable masses behind and forced through the narrow gap created by the explosion were propelled through like a cork out of a bottle.

Within seconds, they realised that fighting them would be futile and they began looking to escape. Empty weapons dropped as they headed to the nearest wall of their barricade, any thoughts of working together forgotten as it became every man for himself. I aimed at one scrambling over the barricade nearest to me, took aim and fired a short burst that punched holes through the roof of the van he was trying to scramble across. He stopped in shock until another burst of fire from me that just missed him persuaded him to try another route.

Others were doing the same, not allowing them to leave. They were going to answer for and pay with their lives for what they had done. I noticed the bodies of some gang members remained unmoving after been fired at. Killed by either a badly or well-aimed warning shot, depending on your point of view.

Everyone who tried to escape I sent scrambling back, bullets flying around their heads as their pleas for mercy fell on deaf ears.

The zombies kept surging through the gap, rapidly filling the square created by the vehicles. I had seen none escape. I did not feel any guilt, they had sealed their own fate when they shot Daniel.

When the line of cars began to buckle, pushed aside like toy cars by the sheer weight of numbers pressing against them, it was time to leave. To get back to the others.

I took a few seconds to watch what we had created, after gathering up my ejected magazines.

The camp was filled with snarling, groaning beasts. One of the gang must have locked himself in a van. It was rocking as it was pushed at from all sides. They wanted the prize that was inside, and nothing was going to stop them getting it.

The van toppled over, crushing some as it fell. I could hear the man's shrill screams of panic, trapped as he was, with no possible means of escape. The windscreen buckled, pushed inwards as it gave way to the snarling faces pressing against it, the screams of terror changing to howls of pain as they reached him and began feasting on his living flesh.

Dave and Simon had left the bridge and called for us to join them back on the road.

"Well done, guys," said Dave. "Let's double-time it back. The back wall of the barricade has already been destroyed by them and it won't be long until they break through the one facing us. We need to get back and find an alternative route around them."

The others had not been idle in our absence. They'd already thoughtfully dug a grave for Daniel and laid his body in it. We gathered round as the Vicar conducted a brief but emotional service at his graveside and we all said our last goodbyes.

Following that, and in the time it took us all to board all the vehicles, Simon quickly went to retrieve his trailer that we'd abandoned earlier. Starting our engines, we followed Shawn as he led the way back down the motorway to find a route around the impassable mass of the undead.

Forty-two people and one dog silently kept watch for the next threat as they continued the journey. The dog not so much, he was asleep again.

CHAPTER ELEVEN

The route Shawn chose took us back over the same bridge we had just been on. We couldn't help but slow down and gawk like rubberneckers reducing speed to look at a crash on another carriageway as they passed it. The barrier of cars had been destroyed by the advancing zombies, their weight of numbers unstoppable. Still stretching into the distance, the compact mass of countless thousands continued their journey south in their search for their next meal.

At Weston-super-Mare we'd been forced to divert off the motorway when we'd found it blocked by a vast mangle of crashed and abandoned vehicles and thousands of zombies. If they kept on going straight and didn't deviate from the obvious straight route, they would eventually meet. Joining together, and if they kept going, their eventual destination would be the end of the motorway at Exeter, and from there following the same route we had taken, but in the opposite direction deeper into the southwest towards Cornwall.

I thought of Willie. Would he remain safe, protected by his isolation in the wilds of Dartmoor? If we had a Ham Radio, we could contact him and warn him.

Shawn was already on the lookout for CB radios to scavenge from trucks, but we also needed to look out for the tell-tale signs of a house with a radio antenna rigged up on the property some-where and take it.

Had the soldiers found their families safe and well? The chances, I knew, were slim and with the massive pack of undead slowly heading their way, I also hoped they wouldn't encounter them. Despite their armoured vehicles and firepower, their only chance of survival would be to avoid them, retreat and only pick fights they could win.

***

Dartmoor

In the days following the group's departure, Willie worked tire-lessly, reinforcing and improving his perimeter; building walls higher, adding extra barriers of wire fences and more early warn-ing trip wires and flares. Being alone, he knew it was impossible for him to maintain an effective all-round guard, so he ensured that what he built and improved would offer him the best protec-tion.

The house he turned into a fortress, strengthening the shutters and keeping the now heavily armoured tractor and trailer parked up against its wall so if need be, he could climb down from an upper window and escape.

He built defensible outposts around his property and further afield. Places he could keep watch from or run to if caught una-wares. Hidden in each was a small stash of food and extra ammu-nition.

Already a very organised man, he catalogued his food and equipment supplies. Augmented by his foraging and hunting skills, he knew he could survive indefinitely at his farm. If he took people in, though, as he had promised and was prepared to do, the extra mouths would eventually put a strain on his resources.

Using his intimate knowledge of the moors from his years living on them, he began patrolling further field. Visiting the nearest properties to him first, he quickly became adept at dispatching the previous occupants if they were still 'living' there, taking any food or other supplies he found back to his property.

The trip to the nearest shop nearly ended in disaster when the hotel and pub that was next door to it spewed out a crowd of zombies attracted by the noise he'd made breaking into the shop. A few desperate minutes ensued as he hacked, punched and kicked his way through the enveloping horde.

His stubbornness refused to let him be beaten by them, though. Nothing would stop him completing the task he had set himself. An hour later, he had hunted down and killed every last one of them, gaining knowledge at every kill about the nature and capabilities of his new enemy. It took him the rest of the day to empty the shop and transport what he needed home.

When darkness forced him indoors, he sat in his usual chair and planned the following day's missions and targets. He had always been contented living alone on the moors, happy with his own company, never imagining for even a moment that he would want to share his peaceful, happy, but solitary existence with anyone.

And then Maud came along.

Loneliness was a feeling he had never experienced before, but he found his thoughts often turning to her and the rest of the group that had sought shelter at his farm for a few short days. Eventually he came to realise that the physical pangs he was feeling and the sense of emptiness in his heart was disappointment. He had missed an opportunity. One that had never happened before to him and one that as far as he knew, would not fall to him again.

He missed them, the companionship and camaraderie that had made his home come alive again. It reminded him of what he missed about his time serving in the armed forces; a sense of family.

But most of all he missed Maud.

When she'd asked him to join them he had refused without hesitation, content to remain in the nice peaceful existence he had created for himself.

A decision he now regretted.

Not being one to dwell on regrets, he forced himself to put those feelings aside and continue with his new mission and goal in life. To seek out and offer help to anyone he could.

The problem was he had not found a living soul yet. He had found evidence of people camping recently on the moors and on one occasion on the edge of the moors, found the still smouldering and glowing remains of a camp fire and evidence of a hastily departed overnight rough camp. He followed the trail, hoping to find his first survivors.

Zombies scattered the path, evidence of a bitter fight for survival. Re-killed, and from what Willie could tell, it had happened recently. Willie quickened his pace, hoping he could reach them in time to help.

He found them a mile later. They had attempted to reach one of the granite tors that towered from the ground in many places over the moors, seeking the safety the castle-like rocks could provide. This one, unfortunately, had sides too steep to climb and they had become trapped, forced into a small cleft in its side. Zombies littered the ground around the entrance, all with their heads smashed in from whatever weapons they had been carrying. One he noticed still had a golf iron with a broken shaft sticking from its skull. The loss of the weapon had sealed their terrible fate. At the end of the narrow cleft three zombies were still feasting on the bodies.

Willie's anger grew. The family had almost made it, killing over twenty in their desperate fighting retreat, only to have their main weapon break with only three left to fight. The whole unfairness of it turned his anger into rage. He had almost found his first survivors, he could have offered them shelter and safety, a chance to live.

Instead, he had missed them by probably no more than thirty minutes. The rage increased as he began to feel guilty. He had let them down. Why hadn't he left earlier that morning? He'd selfishly sat having a second cup of coffee, waiting for the dawn to show itself on the horizon, while this family was fighting for its existence.

He let his rifle drop on the harness that held it to his body and pulled the adapted light sledgehammer he'd chosen as his preferred close quarter weapon from the straps that held it to his pack. One end of the head he had sharpened with an angle grinder for use as a piercing weapon, the other he'd left as a blunt head smasher. It was light enough so when it was swung it didn't unbalance him, but still had enough weight to it to make it deadly. Still feasting on their latest victims, the three zombies hadn't noticed Willie. Previously he had always, out of some inbuilt sense of fairness, got the attention of any zombie he was going to kill, enabling him to attack them face to face and not in his opinion, in cowardly fashion from behind. This time he did not afford them that luxury and stepping forward into the narrow opening in the rock, he swung his weapon hard overhead time after time, the blood and brains from their smashed heads and bodies splashing up the rock in some macabre new version of a cave painting. Eventually, with his anger subsiding and his rage spent, he stepped, panting from the exertion, from the cool shade cast by the rocks into the bright sunlight shining over the moors.

Sitting down heavily on a rock, he took a long pull from his water bottle before reaching into his top pocket, retrieving, and lighting a fresh cigar.

He sat, enjoying the silence and looked over from his elevated position across the moors he loved, and which had been his home for decades. The exhaled smoke from his cigar slowly drifted and dissipated in the light wind that provided only slight relief from the growing heat.

He pondered his next step.

In his days of searching, he had found no survivors. The fact he had just missed out on saving some broke his heart and he began to question the futility of his promise. Did this mean that all he would keep finding would be the grizzly remains of more unlucky ones? Could he stay strong enough to cope with that?

It was summer, and the moors would be an obvious choice for any still in the area to escape to. Winter, though, would be a different story. In a few short months they would change from the beautiful, wild and remote place they were now to a bleak, desolate and inhospitable environment. A place where even those with advanced survival skills would question the sense of attempting to live for any period of time. If any were heading to the moors, he was sure they would have done so by now.

Wille could survive. He was used to the conditions and he had a roof and a warm fire to make himself comfortable. The conditions, he knew, would curtail his ability to patrol a wide area, forcing his world to shrink to a small radius around his farm and isolating him even further from the outside world be was beginning to realise he now missed.

As he sat, pulling on his cigar, lost deep in thought, he slowly reached the conclusion that had been bouncing around in his head for the past days.

His future was not on the moors, it was with Maud.

The daunting journey didn't worry him, he would make it or die trying.

Decision made, he stood up, made sure all his kit was securely in place and strode off across the land to his farm.

He hoped he would not be alone for much longer.

CHAPTER TWELVE

Willie

Crossing the Moors, Willie maintained a pace that would have broken many younger, fitter people. He had a new mission and he was eager to start it as soon as possible.

A sound came to him, carried on the wind. A distant but familiar 'rat tat tat' and popping sounds faded in and out.

Knowing instantly it was gunfire, not just normal gunfire, but a machine gun firing, meant one thing to him.

Military!

The long-sustained bursts also meant they were heavily engaged, and in this day and age, that also meant only one thing: zombies.

Standing still and listening to the distant sounds, he worked out the approximate direction they were coming from. They were at least over two miles away by his reckoning. Closer to the edge of the moors. A few villages and hamlets were in that direction. It could be coming from any of a number of locations.

Willie took a drink from his bottle, tightened the straps on his Bergen and checked the other equipment he carried wouldn't come loose and hamper his progress.

Muttering to himself, "Shall we see what's going on then, laddie?" he started to jog towards the distant sounds, picking up the pace as his muscles warmed and his Bergen settled on his back.

***

Captain Hammond

Firing single shots from the window of the Armoured vehicle, he aimed at the heads of the zombies nearest to him, blood and brains spraying from the back of their destroyed skulls as they fell to join the growing mound of bodies that surrounded the desperate position they found themselves in.

He changed magazines and looked around, then smashed his fist against the front windscreen and screamed in frustration.

The rear vehicle of their convoy, a lorry, was stuck, jammed against a wall with its rear wheels raised off the ground by a built-up morass of crushed and mangled bodies. It was engulfed by zombies trying to reach the two soldiers inside. The other vehicles were similarly surrounded. Fortunately, every vehicle they had taken from the base at Cheltenham had upgraded protection built into them, so as long as the men stayed inside their vehicle, they would be protected by the armoured glass and reinforced sides and doors.

The higher level of the lorries and the armoured car still allowed the men to fire down on the zombies, but the men in the lower slung Land Rovers had to endure being trapped with the zombies pressing right up to the windows, enveloping them under a mass of flesh as they climbed up and onto the bonnets and roofs

Stuck for over half an hour, they were now just firing occasionally at the zombies surrounding them. Not with any hope of being able to rid themselves of them, but out of a sense of frustration, of at least doing something rather than sitting there helplessly watching the milling undead.

"When is something just going to go right for us? Come on, please, give us one break, I beg you."

He had hoped that after their first desperate days their situation would improve. First of all, they'd found themselves battling through the streets of Cheltenham until forced to shelter in a house for days until the horde moved on, enabling them to get back to their base.

No one was left alive at the base and with no command contactable to get further orders, they had chosen to try and reach their families based at a barracks near Exeter.

Taking what they wanted from the vehicle pool and loading them with everything they could take from the armoury, they formed a convoy and headed south.

Hopes were raised when they met the group led by a few Marine Sergeants, heading north in a ragtag convoy of heavily adapted civilian and farm vehicles. If they had survived, then their families might still be alive.

Only to have those hopes smashed when they reached the barracks.

The family housing area had no real fences to keep out the hordes from the nearby city and was completely overrun. He lost more men as they, overcome by the desperate need to reach their families and blind to the dangers they faced, left the relative safety of the vehicles and tried to find their loved ones.

He had watched, horrified, as more of his command fell to the masses as they futilely tried to fight their way through, screaming the names of their wives and children until the screams changed to screeches of agony and failure.

It took every ounce of his strength of personality and persuasive skills to hold the remnants of his unit together. To make them stay in the vehicles and not leave, as they wanted to do. They slowly drove through the housing estate, the power of the armoured vehicle crushing everything in its path. But they found no one alive.

One soldier could not take the sight of his wife and daughter, both bearing terrible wounds, feeding on the remains of what had once been his friend and neighbour in the front garden of what had been their home. Before anyone could stop him, he lifted his pistol and blew his brains all over the rear of the armoured vehicle.

He kept a wary eye on his men from then on.

Barrels glowed red hot from continuous firing as they drove slowly round and round the estate, blaring their horns and using the PA system on the armoured car, pleading to anyone who might still be alive to signal any way they could that they still lived.

Every few hundred yards they stopped, turned off their engines and in the relative quiet, a quiet only disturbed by the raspy growls and groans of the zombies following their route like the Pied Piper leading the rats from Hamlin, they listened. Straining their ears, they fruitlessly tried to identify shouting or banging coming from anyone who could hear them but could not leave their hiding place.

Realisation eventually came to them all. Their families and friends had not survived. Some may have escaped, but to where? They'd spent hours searching and hadn't found anyone alive.

The hard and bitter truth was that they were too late. They'd arrived in hope but had only found death. If any had managed to escape, finding them would be like looking for a needle in a haystack, because they could be anywhere.

Captain Hammond was at a loss what to do next. He had led his men south to reunite them with their families, but that was not going to happen now. He felt useless, berating himself for not being able to fulfil their goal. Blaming himself for the needless deaths of more of his men when he lost control of them and they left the vehicles to search for their families.

His career in the military had been, until now, going to plan. Performing well in his various postings, he was confident promotion and advancement would only be a matter of time. The zombie outbreak had been his first fighting command and he had failed completely, unable to save most of his men and reduced to the rank of spectator as he watched them being ripped apart.

Why hadn't he thought ahead about what his men might do when they reached the base? He should have known how they might react and planned a way to keep them in the vehicles.

He could have prevented another death when the poor soldier unable to cope with the knowledge that he hadn't been there to protect his family had taken his own life.

The enormity of his failings hit him like a brick wall. He wasn't fit to be in command, he didn't deserve to even live when so many of the men he was supposed to lead had died.

Slumping back in his seat, he stared at the chaos surrounding them. Pulling his sidearm from its holster, he stared at it for long seconds, tears of shame filling his eyes.

His sergeant, who was driving the vehicle glanced over at him. Noticing the pistol in his hand and the tears that were falling onto it as he stared at it.

Stamping on the brakes, the vehicle juddered to a halt.

With a shout of, "Don't you fucking dare, Sir!" He reached over and grabbed the gun from his hands.

Dazed, the captain turned to look at him.

"I'm sorry Sarge, I've failed all of you. I am not fit to command anyone."

"The hell you aren't, Sir. If it wasn't for you, we would all have been dead long ago. Why do you think we are the only ones to have made it? Because of you, that's why. You got us out of Cheltenham. You kept us together. Every time it mattered, you made the right decision. You led, us SIR! Don't quit on us now. The lads need you more than ever now. Goddammit, I need you. Without you we won't stand a chance."

Captain Hammond stared long and hard at his Sergeant, digesting what he had said. The following zombies had caught up with them by now and the vehicle rocked slightly as they pressed up against its sides, hands just able to reach the window, clawing at the armoured glass windows.

"Sorry, Sarge. You're right. It just caught up with me there. I won't let it happen again. And as for you needing me. Bloody hell, man, you have far more active service under your belt than me, it's you we should really be taking orders from, not some bloody upstart Rupert like me."

The sergeant laughed.

"That's more like it, Sir. We all know that's not how it works in the Queen's Army. My job is to offer suggestions to my superior officer and stop the young gentleman in question thinking he's bloody Montgomery. As long as he occasionally listens to that advice, we should all get along fine."

"Okay then, Sarge. What do you suggest we do now?"

"First of all, Sir. I would respectfully request we get the fuck out of here. There ain't no one left and driving around in circles is just burning fuel and wasting ammunition. We need to find somewhere to rest up for a few days.

Then, do you remember that guy the other group told us about on the moors? Willie was his name, I think. His location sounds just the place we should head for to get our shit back together again. Everyone is dead on their feet, we can't go on much longer without some proper rest. After that? Well, you're in charge, so I'll let you come up with something."

Captain Hammond immediately reached for a map. He located the moors and stared at the sheet. After a few seconds, he turned to the sergeant.

"I don't suppose you made a note of the grid reference of his farm, did you?"

"Oh no, Sir. I'm a mere Non-Com and as such rely on my superiors to read something as complicated as a map."

He reached over and pointed to a spot on the moors.

"But if I were you, Sir, I think that's as good a spot to head to as any."

He grinned at the captain. "Come to think of it, the Marine Sergeant may have shown me when we were having a chat."

"Thank you, Sergeant. Now if you would be so kind as to radio the other vehicles that we are getting the hell out of here while I plan the route?"

The convoy started its engines and slowly followed the armoured car as it pulverised any zombie that got in its way.

All guns fell silent as the soldiers looked sadly at the housing area that had been their home for the last time. It had been home for their families and loved ones, their children had gone to the local school here. They had played in the park and drunk at the local pub. They had kissed their wives goodbye every time they were deployed, usually with tears from them as they watched their men leave, maybe never to return. Such was Army life.

But now the more dangerous posting had been to stay. They were alive where their loved ones had perished.

More than one tear was shed as they watched the estate, along with their former lives, fade into the distance.

The captain had not left a wife or girlfriend behind, but he could guess what emotions his men must be going through. Survivor's guilt would probably be the best way to describe it.

He talked softly through the radio, trying to reassure his men that they would survive, promising them that the deaths of their loved ones would not be in vain and would be avenged.

Unsure if his words were having the right effect, he stopped and asked his Sergeant if he should continue.

"It doesn't matter what you say, Sir. These men need leadership now more than any time in their lives. It is you they will look to for it, not me. Just keep talking to them, tell them where we're going and so on. Anything to keep their minds away from the rest of the crap that's going on."

And he did.

As the Sergeant followed the route he had shown him, the Captain kept an eye out for a place to stop. A sign for an industrial estate caught his attention, so he told the Sergeant to head towards it. Finding the whole area deserted, he cut through a padlock on the gate to what looked like a transport depot and the convoy followed the lead vehicle as it drove in. Pulling the gate closed and securing it again, he jogged to catch up with his men.

Leaving the machine guns manned, the remains of his command disembarked from the vehicles and did a complete sweep of the area to make sure no surprises lay in wait. The vehicle maintenance area was in a large steel shed with a metal sliding door, which could easily house all their vehicles and with the main door closed, it would give them a secure area further protected by a sturdy perimeter fence.

As soon as the shutter was closed, in the dim light coming through the skylights, the exhausted men turned off their engines and gathered together.

The captain addressed his men, trying to bolster their spirits. An impossible job when taking into account what they had been through.

Rest was what they needed more than anything. Despite his own exhaustion, he knew sleep would not find him easily, so he took the kindest action he could think of for them. He ordered them to stand down completely and he would take watch.

His men individually and silently went to find a place to bed down, each lost in his own grief and heartbreak. In the advancing gloom, the captain listened to the quiet moans, snores and occasional sobbing emanating from various places around the room.

Six hours later, his Sergeant relieved him and despite his protests, forced him to get some sleep himself.

He slept for eighteen hours straight.

They stayed in the unexpected sanctuary for three days before he felt his men were ready to continue the journey. The enforced quietness and calm gave them the chance they needed to absorb and deal with their emotions. They spent their time either alone, cleaning their weapons and kit, or tinkering with and doing basic maintenance and servicing all the vehicles. Rebuilding and strengthening the bonds that would make them an effective fighting force once more.

Ensuring the gate was secure, they headed to the moors to find the man who they hoped would offer them shelter and safety in the depths of Dartmoor.

Following the planned route, they slowly felt their way towards the moors via as many backroads as possible, hoping to avoid any undead that might delay their passage. It went well until they had to cross the only main road that traversed their route. The moors could be seen rising ahead, which meant they were closing in on their destination, but it also meant there were fewer roads to choose from. Only a small number of roads crossed the moors and even though they could use sideroads for another mile or so, eventually they would have to join the main road that cut through them.

Stopping at that junction, they found it thick with zombies, all shambling along in the same direction.

With no other option, Captain Hammond gave the order to plough through them and to keep following the intended route, thinking they would soon leave them behind as they continued.

The plan came apart when they entered the village not far from the main road.

Unfortunately, the way ahead was blocked by a lorry. It must have crashed at some speed into a house alongside the road, because a good portion of the house had collapsed, blocking the way ahead.

A quick scan of the map revealed an alternative route. They just needed to turn around and backtrack a few hundred yards to join a road which should take them on another route through the village and around the blockage.

The problem was that they had attracted the unwanted attention of the zombies when crossing the main road, and they appeared as a solid wall of terror, blocking the way to their new route. The armoured car would have been able to smash through them, but that was now at the wrong end of the convoy.

The lorry bringing up the rear tried to reverse through them but the bodies all too quickly piled up underneath it, forcing it to lose control and crash into a wall, where it now lay stuck, blocking their escape route.

Shaking the pain from his hand after smashing it against the windscreen of the armoured car, he looked to his Sergeant.

"I believe this is just about the right time for you to come up with a brilliant suggestion, Sergeant."

He waited for the heavy calibre machine gun in the rotating cupola on top of the armoured car to finish another long burst. The bullets had the power to destroy many until stopped by something more solid than flesh and bone. Each burst cut a massive swath through the undead, and depending on where it hit bodies, disintegrated or arms legs or heads flew in all directions. The relentless horde soon filled these gaps, though, and continued gathering around them in ever increasing numbers.

"Hate to say it, Captain, but I'm all out of ideas for now. But we could ask that person waving what I think is a bed sheet at us through that window over there."

He pointed a finger over the heads of the zombies crowding around them at a building across the road. The window was closed, and the person couldn't be seen, but a white sheet was indeed being waved up and down in it, trying to attract their attention.

CHAPTER THIRTEEN

Willie

Willie was breathing hard and sweat was pouring down his face, but he forced himself to maintain the punishing pace he'd set.

The gunfire was getting closer with every step and the last thing he wanted was to arrive too late to help. The firing had slowed, but not stopped, which to him probably meant that probably there were either fewer people firing, or they were running low on ammunition; neither scenario much good if they were surrounded by zombies.

He only slowed the pace as he neared the village. Not out of tiredness, but as a practical move. The last thing he wanted to do was to rush into a situation he had no tactical awareness of. Now he was there, the last few hundred yards would need to be slow and cautious. Zombies were in the area and bullets were also still outgoing. Getting shot or being on the menu was not something he wanted to happen to himself for the sake of a bit of caution.

The village wasn't large, so it didn't take him long to creep through back gardens and climb over fences until he knew he was at the rear of a large house that faced the main road that went through it.

Finding the back door unlocked, he slowly entered, his senses on high alert, ready to face anything he found, alive or not, still occupying it. Not discovering anything, he cautiously made his way upstairs and found a room that overlooked the front.

Still mindful of incoming fire, he crawled to the window and raised his head over the sill, had a quick glance and ducked back down again.

That quick look told him all he needed to know. He had discovered a small military convoy that had become immobilised by some unlucky circumstance and now found themselves trapped by a milling crowd of thousands of the undead.

He needed to help them, but how?

Shrugging himself free from the weight of his Bergen and retrieving his water bottle, he took a drink from it as he sat with his back against a wall, got his breath back and came up with a plan.

The first thing he needed to do was to get their attention. With so many zombies out there, it was impossible for him to reach them or vice versa. Another burst of fire from the trapped soldiers made him wince. If they kept making so much noise, there was no way they would disperse. Yes, they were killing some with every bullet fired, but all it was doing was advertising their presence to any within hearing distance. And those guns were loud and could be heard from a long way off. If they kept it up, he might find himself trapped soon.

Pulling a bedsheet from the bed next to him, he tied it to his rifle and keeping his back against the wall, just in case a nervous trigger finger decided he was a new target, he began waving it up and down in front of the window.

Minutes went by with no reaction. There was nothing else he could think of doing to get their attention, so he just had to keep at until they noticed him.

When he was about to give up and try and come up with something else, the loudspeaker on the vehicle screeched and a voice boomed out across the village.

"You in the window. We see you. Are in in a position to offer us assistance?"

Lowering his rifle and removing the sheet, he peered round the window.

The machine gun in the turret of the lead armoured car was now facing him and a rifle was pointing out of the window in his direction.

He was not a coward by any means, but the idea of showing himself while facing a big machine gun that looked like a fifty cal and another automatic rifle, did not fill him with joy. But he decided where else would they be pointing their weapons, and anyway the machine gun could reduce the room he was standing in to rubble in a matter of seconds, so the false security of the wall he was using for protection did not mean that much, really. Slowly and with his hands held out to show he wasn't holding a weapon, he stepped in front of the window to show himself.

After a few seconds with no incoming fire, he relaxed a bit and raised his arm in the universal sign of hello.

"Are you military?" boomed the voice over the loudspeaker. "How many are you?"

Willie was dressed in army surplus clothing, so the assumption was a logical one to make. He slowly shook his head to signal he was not and held up one finger to tell them he was on his own.

A plan had been forming in his mind. He first needed them to be quiet, so he could begin.

Using more basic hand signals he told them to be quiet and to wait.

Hand signals taught in the military hadn't changed much over the years, therefore, these basic instructions were easy to get across.

Acknowledgment was even easier using the vehicle's PA system.

"Understood," came the reply. "We'll go quiet and wait."

Giving them the thumbs up, he stepped away from the window, pulled on his Bergen and exited the house. The idea he was forming was to create a noisy diversion a short distance away, which he hoped would get the horde to move on.

With not much more of a plan than that, he slowly worked his way through the village, using his hand weapon to pulverise the brains of the few zombies he came across that had wandered away from the main crowd.

Spotting a house on the edge of the village that stood in the middle of a large plot, he decided to see if he could find inspiration there to begin the rescue mission.

His plan became more solid when he noticed the propane tank that supplied the house with gas in the garden. What would be better for getting the zombies' attention than a big bang!

Peering through the kitchen window of the house, to his dismay he could see the former occupants in the kitchen. None had any visible injuries, but they had clearly turned. Without any distractions they were all standing in the large kitchen, their heads bowed as if in a trance. In hibernation, as it were, until the chance came to satiate their hunger for human flesh.

Willie hadn't had to kill any zombie children yet. He'd known the time would come, but so far all he had come across were adults. He'd seen the horrific chewed remains of youngsters, but not any 'live' ones.

"Come on, laddie," he said quietly to himself, preparing himself to do what went against all the laws of decency and moral conduct he had tried to live his life by: harming children.

Finding the kitchen door unlocked, he quietly opened it. Quickly rechecking that all his gear was in place and wouldn't hamper him, he tapped his weapon against the door frame to get their attention.

Four heads snapped in his direction. Low groans and growls issued from four throats as four pairs of eyes transfixed him. The nearest one, the husband and father, seemed to smell the air, as if relishing the smell of fresh human flesh emanating from Willie's body, before groaning louder and moving to the open door. His loud rasping call and movement was the command for the rest of the pack, his family, to follow him and feast on the meal that had appeared at their door.

Willie stepped back from the doorway and raised his weapon, ready to strike. Previous experience had taught him that if you killed the first one, the ones behind wouldn't step over or around the carcass, but would invariably still take the most direct route and stumble over it in their need to get to you.

The man reached the door and paused, trying to locate Wille, who had stepped a few paces back. Knowing this was the time to strike, Willie swung his sledgehammer overhead, the blunt end smashing straight down through his head, leaving an unrecognisable, deformed mess of blood, bones and hair as he dropped to the floor, half-blocking the doorway.

The remainder of the family were easy to kill as they predictably fell over the body and lay sprawling in the doorway, their arms and legs moving without coordination as they tried to regain their feet. Willie was thankful the children had fallen face first, so he didn't have to look at their faces as he swung his weapon at their exposed heads.

Dragging the limp corpses out of the way to avoid stepping over them, he entered the house. His plan was as all the best ones were: simple. Turn the taps on the oven to release the gas and leave something burning somewhere so when the gas reached it, it should ignite and cause an explosion. He just needed to make sure he wasn't near it when it blew.

Making sure all the downstairs windows and external doors were closed, apart from the kitchen, he searched through the kitchen drawers till he found what he was looking for: some candles. He knew that the propane in the gas tank outside was heavier than air, and so, when he left the house and closed the door, the escaping gas would build up, filling the downstairs of the house slowly like an invisible flood. Opening the doors to all the internal rooms in the house to allow the gas to spread throughout the ground floor, he set the candles near to the top of a bookcase in the hallway, putting them in some handily left ornamental candlestick holders to ensure they wouldn't fall over, and then he lit them.

In the kitchen, he turned on all the gas taps to the hob and oven and waited for a minute to make sure the gas kept flowing and that it didn't just stop. He knew some cookers had an auto cut-off safety feature, but fortunately, this wasn't one of them. Once he was sure, he left, closing the door behind him.

After making his way stealthily back to the house overlooking the convoy, he got their attention again. Despite the military contingent going quiet and hunkering down in their vehicles, the zombies had not wandered far and were still pressed tightly against all the vehicles.

The ones in the armoured cars and lorries were okay as the zombies couldn't see them in their elevated positions, but they still clawed at the sides of the vehicles. Wille thought, though, that it must be an uncomfortable experience for the ones in the Land Rovers. The zombies pressed their faces up to the windows, inches from their own, teeth and hands continually trying to break the bullet proof glass that provided the only protection.

Signalling to them to hold fast and wait, he moved away from the window to avoid being inadvertently spotted and sat with his back against the wall and waited.

Ten minutes later he was beginning to doubt his plan would work. He thought that surely the gas level should have reached the candle flame by now and began to wonder if the candles had gone out or if there had been enough gas in the tank.

Staring at his watch, he decided to give it five more minutes, and then he would have to decide what to do next.

It would be stupid to return to the house to check, he knew that, so he would have to come up with another plan to get the zombies to move on.

He was muttering to himself a few minutes later as he got to his feet, "Well done you idiot, better come up with plan B, then," when suddenly his breath was completely knocked out of him and he was thrown across the room by a huge explosion. The window shattered, covering him with glass.

Lying stunned with his ears ringing, it took him a few moments to gather his senses and realise that his plan had worked. Struggling back to his feet and wiping blood from a cut above his eye, he staggered to the window that was hanging by one remaining hinge from its frame.

Almost every zombie had been knocked off its feet. All the windows as far as he could see in the village had been shattered by the force of the blast. Looking towards where the house had been, a huge mushroom cloud was slowly climbing into the sky, the top of it dissipating as the wind caught it.

Willie chuckled to himself, "Oops. Think you overdid it a bit there, my boy."

The zombies slowly regained their feet and as one, they began to move towards the source of the explosion, the crackling flames and the huge pall of rising black smoke acting as a beacon for them. When the last zombie had shambled from view, he made his way to the front door and opened it.

He was going to be alone no longer.

CHAPTER FOURTEEN

Captain Hammond

"What do you think he's up to?" whispered the captain to his Sergeant as they sat as low down in their seats as they could to avoid agitating the zombies that surrounded them.

"Not a clue, Boss. But what other choice do we have? He seemed to have a plan and my money is on him being ex-forces. All we can do is wait and see what he comes up with."

Time dragged as they sat there, the vehicle despite its weight being rocked by the undead pushing against it.

When he returned to the window and signalled them to wait, they could do little else but comply.

The blast, when it occurred, took them completely by surprise. The vehicle jumped as it was lifted on its axles and bounced around as it settled again.

Captain Hammond was thrown from his seat and ended up in the footwell. Scrambling back up, he could see the damage the explosion had caused. Curtains flapped from empty, shattered windows and most of the zombies were clumsily trying to stand back up again after being knocked flat by the force of it.

His thoughts immediately turned to his men. The one in the back of the armoured car was shaken up but okay. The Land Rovers had been swept clean of the zombies that had climbed on to the bonnets and roofs by the blast wave, and he could see the occupants inside moving, so he assumed they were also okay.

"It's working. I haven't got a clue what he did, but it's working," cried out the Sergeant as he noticed the zombies that had regained their feet begin to walk off in the direction of the rising pall of smoke created by the explosion.

"What the hell was that?" muttered the captain as he shook his head, trying to get the ringing in his ears to subside.

"It's what you call a bloody good diversion, that's what that was," laughed the Sergeant as still more zombies began to stream from the centre of the village.

It took over ten minutes for the last to leave and disappear from view. The only ones remaining were the hundreds killed or incapacitated by their shooting, damaged but still live ones writhing on the floor, their bodies too broken to allow them to move.

The door to the house opened and their unknown saviour cautiously stepped out and made his way over to them, using his sledgehammer to end the struggles of any that were close to him.

Seeing him coming towards them, Captain Hammond told his men in the vehicles to keep a good look-out, and he and his Sergeant stepped from the vehicle to meet him.

Willie came to attention and saluted the Captain before extending his hand. Returning the salute and accepting the proffered hand, the Captain spoke first.

"Thank you. We were in a bit of a bind there and frankly we were all out of ideas. You have, and I'm not exaggerating, saved our lives. I owe you a great debt."

"Och Sir. I couldn't very well leave you, could I?" Willie replied, "I've been scouring the moors for days now and you're the first live ones I've come across. I was beginning to think I was the only one left alive around here. I promised friends I would help any I found, so all I was doing was that. Anyway, Sir, what brings you here?" The Sergeant butted in.

"Wait a minute. You're Scottish, you fit the description Sergeant Wood gave us. You don't happen to be a certain Willie Beedie, do you? If so, you're the reason we're here."

A shocked look came across Willie's face.

"What?" he stammered, "How? How the hell do you know my name? You know Woody?"

The captain laughed. "You are Willie Beedie?"

"Yes, Sir."

"You are the reason we are here." He then explained quickly how they'd met Sergeant Wood and the others, days ago on their journey south. Willie held up his hand half-way through his story and interrupted his flow.

"I want to hear this, but do you think it would be a good idea to finish it off at my place? Just one thing, though. How was Maud?"

"Yes, of course," The captain replied and turned to his Sergeant. "Can you see if that lorry can be pulled free? If not, we'll need all hands to empty it."

With a, "Yes Sir," he quickly turned and got to work. "Maud?" Willie's face broke into a huge grin.

"Yes, Sir. That beautiful woman who was most likely protecting the children like a lioness, while keeping the rest of the group behaving in the manner she expects." Smiling at the wistful look that had come across Willie's face when he finished describing her, the Captain assured him that she was in good health and still keeping everyone in line.

Using a chain, one of the Land Rovers, with much revving, screeching tyres and the strong smell of a burning clutch, managed to pull the lorry free from the wall and the mangled bodies that had piled up underneath it. It had sustained damage, one of its rear wheels wobbled and it juddered alarmingly when it moved, but it moved and that was good enough for now. It only needed to last a few miles more.

Zombies could reappear at any time. There was no time to waste, so Willie climbed into the rear of the armoured car and the convoy turned around, found its way around the blocked road and followed Willie's directions to his farm deep in the moors.

Arriving as the sun set on another eventful day, Willie prepared and cooked the first hot meal Captain Hammond and the ten men left under his command had had for a long time.

CHAPTER FIFTEEN

Roused by the delicious smells of bacon frying and coffee, Captain Steve Hammond and his men gathered at Willie's large kitchen table.

Wille was himself refreshed after having his first good night's sleep for days, and he was in a good mood. This was mostly due to Captain Hammond's insisting they did guard duty to give him a night's peace. Singing to himself as he bustled around the kitchen, he heaped bacon, sausages and eggs onto a platter for the men to help themselves from.

The captain noticed that his men seemed in better spirits too. A night sharing stories, discussing the future and drinking fine whiskey in between a not very onerous guard rota to interrupt their sleep, had done wonders. A new chapter had started in their lives, and now they had a mission to take their minds away from the terrible grief that had been looming over them.

Willie had relied on his isolated position being his main defence, but after witnessing the horde that had almost overcome Hammond and his men, he realised that the possibility of an unstoppable mass one day appearing at his walls and fences was something that only luck or fate would decide.

To him, it proved that the decision he had already made to leave was the right one, not just because he wanted to be with

Maud again, but staying could be more dangerous than the journey he was planning.

The soldiers had also agreed in discussions the previous night to accompany him on the journey. With their families gone, there was nothing left to hold them to any particular area. They'd already met this group, and no one could deny that their plan was a sound one.

Captain Hammond had issued no orders and did not influence the decision, knowing that to get them on board with the idea, they all had to agree with this, and indeed any other plan that came up in the future.

Intelligent enough to realise that the unique situation they found themselves in meant the normal rules regarding the chain of command did not apply anymore, he let them all make their own mind up. They were all in this together, after all. He planned to lead them and be responsible for them, but any decision-making process from now on would need to be an 'all ranks' joint agreement for them to remain an effective and cohesive unit.

With the guard rota changing regularly, the men sat round the kitchen table and planned their next move. The agreement having already been reached for them all to head to Warwick Castle, the how and when was what needed to be settled.

Willie dug out a large-scale map from a drawer, and spreading it across the kitchen table, they got on with it. The route was easy to map. They would drive up the M5 motorway, which they already knew was clear as far as Cheltenham, and then hopefully continue onwards until Worcester and then depending on what they found, feel their way across country, either using main or side roads, until they reached Warwick itself.

Choosing what equipment they would take was also easy. Absolutely everything they could!

The real planning was what vehicles they would take. With only twelve of them and six military vehicles and Willie's tractor at their disposal, if they took them all it would leave each one sorely undermanned and difficult to defend. One of them would only have a driver, not an ideal situation at all if any fighting needed to take place.

Wille had converted his tractor and trailer in a similar fashion to the one the soldiers had already seen, and Willie had witnessed first-hand how effective it was at providing something that had the power to smash though zombie masses and also provide an excellent platform to fight from. He insisted that it would be a bad mistake to leave it behind.

Of the three lorries, one was deemed unrepairable given the lack of specialist tools and equipment, so that was as easy one to leave behind. That left the two lorries, two Land Rovers and the armoured vehicle to choose between.

The lorries were essential as they were fully loaded with all the weaponry, ammunition and other supplies taken from Imjen Barracks at Cheltenham. Similarly, the armoured vehicle with its powerful machine gun mounted in the rotating cupola needed to be included.

That left the two Land Rovers. They were armoured so would provide excellent protection, but because of the armour, the windows didn't open. It was never designed to enable guns to be fired from within, and its intended use was merely as a safe patrol vehicle capable of withstanding small-arms fire. Their use in the current situation had already revealed their limitations when surrounded at the village on the edge of the moors only the day before. The soldiers trapped inside could do nothing to help themselves, apart from wait to be rescued.

Both were chosen to be left behind. If they needed more vehicles, they didn't need to be bulletproof, just zombie-proof. Any normal car could be adapted for that purpose and would most likely be more suitable, as they'd seen with what Tom and his group had achieved.

The only unanswered question was whether there would be enough space in the reduced convoy to take not only the load from the lorry they were abandoning, but also the volume of stuff Willie would want to take.

The only way to find out was to get on with it. The twelve men set about their tasks with purpose.

Following Willie's advice, they decided to add the proven wedges and extra protection around all the vehicles, using materials Willie had in one of his outbuildings. The high ground-clearance of all the vehicles made them vulnerable to bodies piling underneath them and either damaging something or grounding them, as had happened with the lorry at the village. Adding sturdy 'skirts' around them would reduce this possibility.

They split into work teams; one to unload the equipment from the disabled lorry, ready to be distributed, and another to work on the vehicles. Willie, with two of the soldiers, created another pile of all the supplies and equipment he wanted to take with him. Both piles looked impressively large. Then Willie went around the outposts he'd built around his property and brought back the supplies and ammunition he'd stashed in each of them, further adding to what needed to be squeezed in.

The willing and skilled hands completed all the work needed by mid-afternoon and they set about loading the vehicles, completing the task as dusk settled over the Moors. There wasn't another inch of space in all the vehicles, and boxes even had to be strapped onto the roofs of the cabs of both the lorries and the tractor.

When the vehicles had been topped off with fuel from Willie's red diesel tank, and the remainder of his tank had been emptied into a towable fuel bowser hooked up to the back of one of the lorries, they were all but ready to depart.

Travelling at night was not something anyone thought sensible, so they settled back into Willie's farmhouse for one last night. Mucking in together to use the last of his perishable goods, they created a delicious hodgepodge which was enough to fill them to bursting and still leave food for breakfast in the morning.

Willie once again produced bottles of whisky from his seemingly inexhaustible supply. The evening mellowed as, between regular patrols, a few more bottles were added to the empties pile building up in the corner.

Captain Hammond had noticed his ham radio set up in the corner of the lounge.

"Have you tried contacting people on it?" he asked.

"Yes, laddie. When it first started, there was plenty of activity, but slowly they all went off the air one by one. I haven't tried it for days, because the silence was too depressing."

"Have you tried any military frequencies?"

"Of course I have," he replied. "I regularly scanned all the usual aviation, emergency and search and rescue frequencies, but never got a squeak."

"Do you mind if one of us has a go?"

"Of course not."

"Corporal Side. You're the radio bunny. Come over here and have a go, please. Willie, the problem we have with the comms we've got is range. We just haven't been able to pick up anything and to be fair, just like you, we've stopped trying. Now, if Corporal Side here can work some magic and use some of that expensive training he's been given, you never know."

Willie bustled around for a few minutes, starting the generator to provide power and making sure the leads were connected correctly before handing the set over to the Corporal.

For the first half an hour, all attention was on him as he tried many and various channels, all to no avail. Slowly, the attention drifted from his efforts and the conversation around the room returned to the tall stories and daft escapades that is the stock the world over for groups of men sitting around a table having a drink.

The Corporal speaking into the handset, stopped all conversation immediately.

Captain Hammond knocked over his chair in his eagerness to get closer to the radio set.

Holding up his hand to indicate he wanted silence, the Corporal carried on talking into the handset. He twiddled with a few more dials and pressed some buttons before turning to his Captain and with huge grin of triumph on his face, said, "Sir, I have the acting Admiral of the Fleet wanting a word with you."

The Corporal vacated the seat and the captain sat down, donned the headphones and picked up the handset.

The men listened avidly to the conversation, and even though they couldn't hear what was being transmitted to them, since only the captain could hear through the headphones, the conversation was easy to follow.

Captain Hammond gave a detailed report of what they'd endured from the first moments they'd received the mobilisation orders in Cheltenham. Once he'd given his report, he spent a long time listening, occasionally confirming he understood what was being said. Eventually, he signed off and removed the headset.

Turning to see every eye was on him, he said.

"Sergeant, call in whoever is on watch. I think everyone should hear this. And can someone get me a bloody whisky, please?"

The moment everyone had gathered, he began.

"Well, gentlemen. That was an interesting conversation. Let me give you the brief version.

What is left of the Royal Navy is currently gathering in the Solent, between Portsmouth and the Isle of Wight. Only ships that were at sea have survived intact. It seems that in the chaos of the first few days, any ships moored in Dockyards or which tried to land to offer assistance, were overcome by the waves of people desperately trying to escape. Unfortunately, before anyone realised what they were dealing with, many infected by bites or the virus had boarded and those ships quickly became butchers' yards and were lost. Hard decisions were eventually made, and the remaining unaffected vessels were ordered to make for open sea, batten down the hatches and not offer any assistance to anyone, no matter the circumstance.

"A few vessels mutinied, their crews unable to accept that they couldn't help their families. Order was eventually restored, but not before some ugly incidents and more ships being lost. Orders have gone out to any of our vessels around the world to make best speed and return home."

He shrugged, taking another sip of his whisky. "And that is the good news!

We are the only contact they've made with any land-based forces still in the field, so to speak. There are a few bases manned with people in bunkers and shelters still communicating, but they all report being unable to leave due to the zombies the other side of their blast doors. They still have access to satellite imagery and communications, but are unable to offer any more than that. Currently, they're trying to carry out a detailed survey to identify any assets left. Early indications are it does not look good.

"All available manpower in the UK was initially dispatched in the first phases of the crisis and quickly became overwhelmed. Aircraft took off but found themselves unable to land when their bases fell to the masses that breached their perimeters. The rest of our Airforce is mainly stuck on the ground, abandoned in bases overrun with zombies.

The long and the short of it is, we are now it. The only known combat effective ground force left in the UK until more ships arrive; they are expecting the helicopter carrier and fleet auxiliary ships to arrive over the next few days, but they can offer us no help. We are still on our own.

On a brighter note they are gathering around them a growing fleet of civilian vessels of all shapes and sizes, and are broadcasting their location over the maritime channels, hoping to attract more who made it to the safety of the sea.

Some of the smaller Channel Islands and maybe the Scilly Isles, are being discussed as future bases and safe anchorages. They are all overrun as the imagery obtained so far shows, but the low populations might make it feasible to clear the islands of the un-dead. A lot of the civilian boats won't be seaworthy enough to last in the open water if a storm rises. Yes, they will be able to shelter in estuaries for the short term, but there are too many people on them to be accommodated on Royal Navy ships. Also, keeping them supplied is a logistical impossibility, even if there are enough stored supplies to go around.

"Anyway, we can't concern ourselves with them for now. The Navy is looking after them the best they can. Our plan to head to Warwick Castle has been endorsed. They'll try to get current images of the location if possible, but can't promise that, because their tasking list is long and full of other priorities. If we get there and it proves to be a secure location, then I believe we can expect more."

He raised his glass to the room, and with all his men avidly taking in every word, he said, "Gents, at first light, we head out in the knowledge that we are not alone. That some remnants of order and scraps of this country that we love have survived. I will not go as far as to say that the country is relying on you, but I will say that *I* am relying on you. Somehow, we will be able to rebuild something from the ashes of the terrible plague that has swept our nation and taken so much from each of us personally."

When he sat down, his Sergeant stood and raised his glass. "Gentlemen. For Queen and country."

They all stood as one and raising their glasses, repeated the toast and downed their drinks.

The volume in the room rose as many conversations broke out, discussing the news.

The Sergeant leant towards his Captain and whispered theatrically,

"You remember my little speech about stopping you becoming Montgomery. Well, Sir, I take it all back. You are him now. Your speech confirmed it, you are the supreme commander of Her Majesty's land forces and until we find a higher ranked officer, the job is yours."

Captain Hammond blinked at the realisation he was probably correct.

"We can't be all that's left, Sarge. There must be others like us?"

"I hope to God there are, Sir but look at the facts. We're the only ones known to have survived from Imjin Barracks. Only four made it from Bickley. If we work on those odds, there can only be a few hundred of us at most. Unfortunately, somehow, I even doubt that. We were lucky and had you to lead us. Every other young officer I've had the privilege to serve under would have got us killed long ago. You have the lucky touch and that goes a long way in my book."

"What do you mean, lucky? Most of my command has been killed, if you remember."

"No, Sir. We are still alive and that's lucky. We met those on the motorway and that was lucky. You navigated us to the Moors to find Willie and found him, that was lucky. You, Sir, have the lucky touch and I'll follow your lead anywhere."

Willie had heard his name mentioned and came over to them, refilling their glasses from the bottle in his hand.

"Sir. Well if all that's true and we are all that's left, I think it is my duty to reenlist and volunteer my services once more. I can't have all you English taking all the glory. The Scots have saved your backsides many times in the past and I'll make sure we will again."

The Sergeant raised his glass to Willie.

"I'd take him, Sir, if I were you. That man, I bet, has seen more action than all of us combined. If he speaks, I would listen."

Captain Hammond also raised his glass in acknowledgment. "Thank you, Willie. I think I'll need all the help I can get.

You've been there, seen it and done it many times. Any contribution you can make will be invaluable, I'm sure. Sergeant Beedie, I accept your reenlistment. Now, if you two Sergeants want to knock your heads together about roles and duties and let me know the outcome, I believe it's my turn on watch."

Picking his rifle up and walking towards the door, both Sergeants watched him.

Willie spoke first as soon as he'd left. "He seems a good one."

"I keep telling him, but I don't think he believes me. I think he thinks it's the usual ego boosting bullshit I need to do to keep my officers on the straight and narrow. But young Steve is one of the best I've come across. He cares for his men and they know it. All he thinks about are his failures not the successes."

He paused for a moment, thinking about the moment when he had grabbed the pistol from his hands, a pistol wet with his own tears and was contemplating using on himself. That would stay between them, something never to be repeated.

He clapped Willie on the back.

"Yep. He'll do, and with us two keeping an eye on him, we'll make a General out of him one day."

Laughing, they joined the rest of the men around the table.

Before turning in for the night, Willie asked Corporal Side to help him dismantle the ham radio set so they could take it with them. It *was* going to be left, but now it was probably one of the most vitally important pieces of equipment they had with them.

Willie lay awake for a while before sleeping, thinking about the years of solitude he had enjoyed on the Moors. He could have been sad if he allowed himself, but the thought of beginning the journey to see Maud again filled him with too much joy.

In the morning he and his eleven new companions would set out on the next stage of their journey.

CHAPTER SIXTEEN

Tom

Carefully approaching the slip road on the next motorway junction we came to, we were relieved to find the way was clear. The horde of zombies had passed and was probably continuing its way southwards, away from us.

Shawn, as usual in the lead, with Louise on the radio warning us of any obstructions ahead, picked up the pace and the miles once again began to slip by.

My car only carried the three of us now. We hadn't had the time to reallocate anyone to Daniel's position in the rear of the vehicle. The car and my clothes were still stained with his blood. I hoped to be able to clean the car soon, otherwise it would continue to be a reminder of the loss we had suffered. I would throw my clothes away as soon as we stopped.

Dave was following our journey on a map, because we needed to know exactly where we were at any one moment, so if need be, we could quickly divert to one of the other routes we had planned if we found another problem ahead.

With his finger following our route, he warned me in advance we were approaching the junction we'd planned to leave the motorway at to reach Louise's parents' home in a small village outside Cheltenham.

I could hear the apprehension in her voice when she told us all to get ready to leave the motorway. She knew, as we all did, that the chances of finding her family alive were remote, but we had promised we would try, and we were fulfilling that promise. I didn't know these people, but I could feel my own nervousness building up. She was one of us now and we all had great empathy for how she must be feeling.

Driving up the off-ramp, I did notice a haze of smoke staining the horizon to the north. Was it an indication of problems ahead? I dismissed it as something we would need to worry about later. Today's destination lay in another direction.

The signs were not good in the few villages we drove through. We were close to Cheltenham, a town we knew had fallen to the zombies on day one of the outbreak. Crashed and abandoned cars blocked the road at times. They proved no problem for Shawn's plough, but it was an indication of the mayhem and chaos that had occurred. Houses lay deserted, with doors open, and contents sometimes strewn around the front garden. Zombies were scattered around the road and gardens, occasionally on their own but mainly in small groups. Attracted by the noise we were making, they stumbled in our direction before falling victim to Shawn's plough or a well-aimed strike from a spear as we passed.

We passed a sign announcing the name of the village we were heading for; a sign that warned us to drive carefully. Shawn slowed down, and turning, we headed up a road that must lead to her parents' house.

Shawn's voice came over the radio as he stopped.

"We're here, guys. I'll pass you over to Dave and Simon."

Dave was standing on the seat of the Volvo, scanning the surrounding area for any danger.

He picked up the radio.

"Simon, it's clear. Do you agree?"

From his different viewpoint he also confirmed he could see no immediate threats.

I stopped the engine and, picking up my rifle, stood up on the seat and looked around.

Louise's parents' house looked deserted, there were no cars on the drive and the front door was closed. A small hedge separated the road from the neat front garden.

Dave ordered us to form the vehicles into the usual square. It took a few minutes and a damaged hedge and flower beds to accomplish, but we all knew what we were doing.

As soon as we were in position and everyone was looking outwards, weapons held ready, Dave gave the all-clear for the assault team to exit the vehicles.

The assault team consisted of all the Marines and knights. The Marines would lead the way but if they found more zombies than they could deal with, they would fall back behind the shield wall and let the knights deal with the threat.

The rest of us would be responsible for looking outwards and stopping any other zombies getting too close.

The door to the bus hissed open and disgorged the fully kitted-up knights. Opening the rear door on the trailer, more knights walked down the ramp and joined them. Now I was getting to know them, even though they were wearing full-face helmets, I could easily distinguish who was who from the size of them, what weapons they carried or the length of the beard draping over their chest plates and chainmail.

Horace wanted to join them and tried to follow Ian as he walked down the ramp. He was a gentle but powerful dog and it took two people holding his collar to stop him. He was eventually tied to a rope, attached to the trailer's side, where he continued barking and whining.

They formed a line surrounding the front door to the house, the Marines holding their rifles ready and standing in front of them.

Louise had exited the cab of the tractor and stood on the platform, where Shawn placed a protective arm around her shoulder.

Simon tried the front door, but finding it locked, he turned to Ian, who stepped forward and aimed his size fourteen feet at the lock. The door crashed open against its hinges.

The Marines cautiously entered the house, followed by the knights, only to return a few tense minutes later.

Dave called to Louise. "It's empty, there's no one home. It all looks neat and tidy; the breakfast dishes are in the sink. No drama happened here, they must have gone out without knowing what was going on."

Louise turned to Shawn. "What day did it all start?"

"It was a Monday, I think," he replied, looking around for confirmation. What day of the week it was had lost all meaning now and we were all losing track of the date.

Becky confirmed it.

"Yes, definitely a Monday."

"They could have gone to the bridge club in the village hall. They never missed it. Most of the retired people in the village go, it's one of the big social occasions of the week."

"How far away is it?" I asked.

"Not far, it's on the other side of the village, by the cricket pitch."

Dave looked at me and I shrugged.

"Okay," he said. "We've come this far, a bit further won't hurt. Let's all get back on board and head to the village hall. But Louise," he warned, "if they aren't there, though, I don't know how much longer we can spend looking."

"No, I understand, and thank you, everyone. If they aren't there, I don't know where else they could be."

Dave raised his voice.

"Right, everyone, back on board and stay sharp."

By the time everyone had got back into their vehicles, a few zombies had started to appear, coming up the road in the direction we had come from.

Shawn spoke over the radio.

"Louise recognises them, they're all neighbours and villagers."

I looked at Dave and said, "This doesn't look good, mate. If we find a room full of zombie OAPS, what the hell are we going to do? Ask nicely for her parents to come out, or are we going to have to kill them all to get the answer she's looking for?"

Dave replied, ending with a quote from the movie *Platoon*, "I hate to say it, but if they are there and have turned, we may not have any other options. It's a lovely fucking war!"

In the few minutes it took everyone to get back on board the vehicles and begin to move off, the zombie villagers reached us. I noticed Louise, as Shawn drove the tractor past me to lead us down the road, crying and pointing at some of them. I couldn't hear what she was saying, but I could imagine her telling Shawn the names of her former neighbours and possibly friends just before he mangled them with the plough.

Driving slowly through the village, the convoy followed Shawn as we headed to the village hall. The car park of the village hall was reasonably full, an indication that Louise was right, and the bridge club had gathered before the apocalypse had hit their peaceful corner of England.

We all drove onto the cricket pitch and formed the usual square of vehicles. I did smile as I noticed all drivers still observed proper etiquette and avoided driving over the hallowed ground of the cricket square.

CHAPTER SEVENTEEN

In the silence after all the engines had been turned off, Dave stood on his seat and addressed everyone. "Same routine as before. The assault team will check out the hall while everyone else keeps watch."

Louise had left the cab and was looking at the car park. "They must be in there. That's their car over there."

The team assembled quickly and exited the protective square of the vehicles and walked towards the village hall.

Horace was still determined to follow his master and was getting more frenetic as he watched Ian leave. Ian turned just before he walked through the tight gap left in the square and asked Becky to let him off the lead.

"The daft mutt can look after himself. Something is making him want to come, so who are we to stop him? He's been cooped up in the trailer all day and he might just want to stretch his legs and do his business."

Horace happily bounced down the ramp the second he was released and after cocking his leg up the tyre of the tractor, followed his master.

Looking at the village hall, I knew that the news was not going to be good. There were streaks of blood on the windows and you could see shadows of figures moving about inside.

Simon and Dave led the men cautiously towards the hall, first approaching a window to look inside. Then they walked in a tight group all the way around it before returning to us.

Dave walked up to Louise, who was standing outside the tractor. Shawn once again stood beside her with a supportive arm around her shoulder.

"I'm really sorry, but everyone inside has turned. The main door opens inwards, so it looks as if they're trapped. If your parents are in there, then they've gone, I'm afraid."

Louise bowed her head and began sobbing. She had known that this mission to find her parents was likely to end in failure and now it had become reality. In the space of a few days she had lost everything dear to her. First she'd had to watch her sister turn and be killed by her own hand thrusting a knife into her diseased brain. She'd been bitten while they were trying to evade zombies. And now her parents were gone too.

Her grief was understandable, and we all stood silently for a while, respecting it.

Eventually she recovered enough to speak, her voice cracking with emotion.

"Thank you, everyone, for trying. At least I know now and can accept and deal with it. What can we do? Do we leave them trapped in there? At least I suppose they're with their friends."

Simon replied.

"Yes. Unless one of them presses against a panic bar on one of the fire doors, which could happen easily, they're trapped. We could block the doors to prevent them, but eventually a window might break, or something could happen, and a door could open."

He paused and looked at the Village Hall before continuing. "It's not worth the risk for us to deal with them. We could consider setting fire to the building. It may sound horrible, but it would stop them from maybe being a problem in the future to any survivors in the area."

Louise looked at the building that housed what had once been her parents and their friends. It was an old building and had probably served as the village hall for generations. It was constructed from both brick and timber and would be old enough for most of the materials used to build it to predate modern construction safety regulations. In other words, it would burn easily.

"I agree. I hate the thought of them remaining in there, but the idea of them escaping, wandering the earth as one of those horrible beasts is even worse. The village hall was a place where they spent a lot of time and it would be a fitting final resting place for them."

The Vicar called over from the trailer.

"I can sanctify the place as holy and perform a funeral service if that will help, my dear. The Good Lord will look after their souls."

"Thank you, Vicar," I said and looked around at the group. "Does anyone have any objections or other ideas?"

No one replied, but many nodded their agreement.

"Right then, that's a plan. Let's get on with it. There are some fuel cans full of petrol in the van, can someone get them, please?" Jamie, standing with his axe over his shoulder, interrupted to point over to the entrance to the carpark. A couple of wandering zombies, obviously attracted by our noisy journey through the village, were approaching, and more could be seen beyond.

"Whatever we're doing, can we get on with it? We're beginning to attract a crowd."

There weren't many of them yet, but as we knew from experience, that situation could change quickly.

Dave turned to me.

"Tom, we can deal with those. You get on with the plan for the village hall."

He turned to the ones looking over the side of the trailer.

"Just make sure a few of you stay on watch and are ready to back us up if we need help, please."

The knights took a few moments to get their pikes from the bus before jogging across the grass with the Marines towards the approaching former villagers. Horace, sticking close to Ian's heels, went too. His hackles raised, he had been growling since before the first ones had appeared.

Shawn's friends had told us how great he'd been when they'd had to fight the huge crowd of zombies that had trapped them inside their house in Bristol. Jumping up and biting the face of one that had clamped its teeth into Ian's chainmail clad arm; getting it off him and keeping him in the fight.

Since we'd met him, he'd growled and barked when zombies were around, sensing them long before they came into sight. Our very own big soft and friendly early warning system.

Chet, carrying two petrol cans he had retrieved from the van, walked up to me.

"How do you want to do this, Tom?" he asked.

"Sensitively, for a start. We must remember that Louise's parents are in there," I replied quietly before turning to look up at the Vicar.

"What do you need to do for this sanctification thing, Vicar? And how long will it take?"

He looked at the approaching zombies.

"Not too long. I'm sure my boss will forgive my brevity, given the circumstances."

He looked at Louise, who was still standing next to Shawn. "My dear, would you like to join me for the ceremony?"

She nodded and climbed down from the tractor. Shawn followed her, and they waited for the vicar to appear from the trailer.

I walked up and gave Louise a quick hug. I caught Shawn's eye and understood the meaning of the look he was giving me, nodding to him the silent response.

"Don't worry mate, I'll watch your back."

The Vicar had taken a few minutes to retrieve some items from amongst his possessions and walked down the ramp wearing his stole, and he was carrying a bible and a few other items.

While we were waiting for him, I chose half of the remaining 'fighters' of the group, asked them to exit their vehicles and led them a small distance away from Louise and Shawn to give them a quick pep talk. Giving them the usual reminders about being vigilant, I made sure that everyone understood what we were trying to achieve, and then we spread out in a protective cordon around the Vicar, Shawn and Louise as they walked over to the Village Hall.

Hearing the Vicar begin reading from the bible and saying prayers, I silently hoped he wouldn't take long. I wasn't following what he was doing very closely, because I was keeping a watch out for approaching threats, but I did notice him make a few signs of the cross and throw what I imagined to be holy water from a small bottle he was carrying in the direction of the building.

From my position I could see the Knights, who with the Marines watching their flanks, were engaging the approaching zombies. They'd formed a line and holding their pikes out, were impaling the heads of any zombie within range. Horace was running up and down in front of them, barking loudly and snapping at hands as they reached out to him.

If one got too close to him, he jumped up at it and sent it flying backwards, often knocking over the one behind it too.

Everyone who had seen Horace fight before was full of praise for his bravery and skill at fighting them and now I could see why. He seemed to intuitively know what was needed and did it unfailingly, really helping the knights as they fought them.

More zombies were gathering than they were able to kill, though, forcing the fighting line to begin to take a step backwards occasionally when the press of bodies became too great. Every step was bringing them closer.

The Vicar was still performing a ceremony. I didn't know if it was the sanctification one or if he'd moved on to the last rites. But whatever he was doing, he needed to get on with it. We still had to set the building alight and make sure it would burn well enough to destroy its inhabitants and render them harmless.

He'd told us his first name was Charles, but it just didn't seem right to use it.

"Vicar," I called, interrupting him mid-prayer, "I hate to say this, but could you hurry it up a bit?"

"One more minute and we will be all done," he replied calmly, without raising his head from the bible, and continued with his service.

Louise was weeping as she stared at the building. I imagined she was trying to see her parents one last time. Shawn, still offering her comfort, was beginning to look uncomfortable at how close the zombies were getting.

The Marines were now helping the knights and shooting down any that threatened to outflank their slow and steady retreat.

Shane, from the trailer, was taking carefully aimed shots at other zombies who were approaching from over the other side of the cricket pitch. I'd noticed them, but in my opinion, the range was too great to take a shot from a standing position with the rifle. If I'd had a rest or a shooting stick to steady my aim, I reckoned I would have been able to make the shot. I'd used shooting sticks a few times before when shooting on a friend's land, and they were a useful piece of equipment when used to help steady your aim and make more consistent shots. I made a mental note to discuss adding them to our zombie-killing inventory. Maybe, I mused, if we combined a spear and a shooting stick together, that could prove a useful tool.

Finally, the Vicar concluded his service. Shawn led the weeping Louise back to the tractor and I called Chet to bring the petrol cans over, so we could set fire to the building.

We didn't need protecting so I told everyone else to report to Dave and Simon to see if they could offer them and the knights some assistance.

Chet had proved his fire-starting skills when he'd set the car alight on the moors to create a smoke screen to cover our journey to Willie's farm.

"Go on, mate," I said to him with a grin. "Don't tell me, you've always wanted to set fire to a building, too. No don't answer that. I might be worried by what you say."

He grinned as he recalled the conversation we'd had just before he set that particular car on fire.

"No, a car was my previous goal, but I reckon I can upgrade to a building, no problem. Do you think you can break one of those windows? If you can, I'll use my knife to put a few holes in the cans, chuck them in, light them and that should do it. It looks as if there are enough tables and chairs in there to catch alight to keep it going."

I walked up to the window and hit the butt stock of the rifle against it. The glass didn't break. I tried a few more times, really putting some weight behind the blows, but the pane still didn't break.

The glass was toughened or laminated and by the feel of it, would probably resist a blow from a hammer.

All my banging on the window had done was attract the attention of those within. They pressed their hands and faces against the glass, lifeless eyes watching our every move. The elderly faces of the village bridge club members did not soften their transparent need to reach us and feast on our flesh, enabling the virus to keep spreading.

Not having a hammer, I used the next best thing. I raised my rifle and fired. The bullet punctured a neat hole in the glass, throwing one of the watching faces backwards as a hole appeared in its forehead.

"Good news," I said to myself. The glass was laminated, i.e. two panes of glass sandwiching a plastic layer, rendering it a lot stronger and resistant to breaking than normal glass. If it had been toughened, the whole pane would have disintegrated. Aiming carefully, I shot out the glass from the lower corner of one of the window panes. Every shot I fired knocked one or more of the occupants over because my bullets were tearing through them as they continued crowding towards the noise I was making. Quickly emptying an entire magazine, I inserted a fresh one and admired my handiwork.

A two-foot by two-foot hole had been blasted into the bottom corner of a window. But now the problem was that the villagers stepping over the bodies of their former friends soon filled the hole in the glass with their clawing, reaching arms, making it impossible to throw the petrol cans in as we had planned.

Looking through the windows, I could see that the entire population of the hall was making its way towards the hole I'd just made. Chet came up with plan B.

"Why don't we do the same at the other end of the hall and chuck in the petrol and light it before they get there?"

Quickly making our way to the other end of the building, we got ready. Chet removed the caps from the two petrol cans and got his knife out, ready to punch some holes in them just before throwing them inside.

Knowing what to do now, it took me no time at all to shoot a hole in the window, emptying another magazine in the process.

The moment I stopped firing, Chet stabbed his knife numerous times into the first can and threw it through the hole in the window. The pungent smell of petrol filled the air as he stabbed the next can and repeated the move. Warning me to stand back, he fetched a box of matches from his pocket and got close to the window.

The ones inside had already begun to move towards the new source of noise we'd created, slowly shambling as one back down the length of the hall, some tripping over the occasional table or chair that hadn't already been pushed out of the way by their continual wanderings.

Chet didn't do as I expected and strike one match and throw it in through the hole in the window. My mind had already registered that the match would most likely go out before it hit the floor to ignite the petrol spilling out of the cans. Instead, he lit one match and, doing something I hadn't done since I was a child, used it to light the rest of the matches still in the box. The box flared and hissed noisily as all the match heads burst into fire in a rapid chain reaction. The box, now emitting a flame over a foot long, was thrown through the hole in the glass by a smiling Chet.

We both stepped back and waited.

Nothing happened for a few seconds. The bodies inside began pressing against the new hole we'd created, arms once more reaching out, hands opening and closing like claws.

Had one of them stepped on the burning matches, putting them out?

When the petrol caught, it did not blow the building up as would happen in Hollywood movies. There was a low whooshing sound and flames appeared throughout the building, following the spreading petrol. Air rushed in through the holes we'd made in the windows as more oxygen was pulled in to feed the flames.

The former villagers had no comprehension of the dangers the flames held and made no move to get out of the way, and either stayed where they were, and the flames caught them up, or they walked towards the new and interesting noise and lights that were spreading across the floor in a blue and yellow flame.

As the first few pensioners caught fire, possibly because the nylon and polyester clothing they were wearing was more inflammable than the natural cotton or wool that others were dressed in, the fire really began to take hold. These human fireballs still walked, not feeling any pain as they bumped into others, setting them alight too. When the curtains caught fire, it was clear the fire was out of control and wouldn't stop until there was nothing left to burn. The whole process had taken no longer than a minute.

Chet and I checked our weapons and ran over to where Dave and Simon were leading the fight against the approaching swarm.

Dave looked at our handiwork. The fire was growing rapidly, and black smoke was pouring from the roof.

"Enjoyed yourselves?" he asked with a grin, before turning back to face the direction the zombies were coming from.

The knights had been working hard and the field in front of them was littered with hundreds of corpses. Facing the massed zombies, shields raised, they screamed their battle cries as they hacked, slashed and thrust at ones trying to climb over a wall of already unmoving corpses.

Looking back across the field, I could see other similarly arranged rows and wondered what tactics they were using.

It wasn't worth asking just then, and I would obviously find out soon enough.

One of them issued a command and they all disengaged immediately and took ten paces backwards. Dropping their shields, they either sheathed or slung their weapons over their backs and reached back to grab a pike from someone who had peeled off from the flanks, picked it up from the ground and held it ready for them.

Another command was issued, and the pikes were lowered, and the knights stepped a few paces forward and formed a line in front of the wall of death they had just created. Breathing heavily, they waited.

The ones who had handed them the pikes went back to the flanks and continued to take shots at any that were spilling from the pack, threatening to outflank them.

"Great work lads," Dave shouted out to them, "One more time, lads and we'll pull back to the vehicles. Knights, when I order it, you peel away and get on board."

"What can we do?" I asked when he'd finished.

He looked around the field. We were about fifty metres away from the vehicles. The village hall was burning fiercely and only a few zombies were approaching from other directions. A shot sounded from the trailer and I watched as another one fell. They were too few to worry about and the others were proving capable of dealing with them.

"We have it sorted here, if you and Chet could take up position halfway between us and the vehicles and keep watch for anything we might miss."

With a nod, Chet and I jogged away to where he indicated and raised our weapons, ready for anything.

I couldn't help myself, though, and kept looking towards where the action was taking place.

It was fascinating to watch.

As soon as the zombies came within range, the knights began killing them with their pikes, every thrust destroying another brain with the sharp spike. The ones killed fell to join the others creating a growing wall of bodies, which when it was high enough, created enough of an obstruction to hold them back.

Horace ran up and down in front of them, knocking over any they missed.

At a shouted command issued from within the solid line of knights, they dropped their pikes behind them and bent down to pick up their shields and reach for their hand weapons. Still all screaming their battle cries, they formed a shield wall and stepped towards the mound of their recent victims and began thrusting, stabbing and hacking again at the ones trying to climb over the obstacle, creating an even higher pile of bodies.

Horace then began patrolling up and down their line, just behind them. Ready to jump in and help if required.

While the knights were busy fighting, Dave got three people to gather up the pikes and take them back to the trailer. Once they'd passed them up, they returned to cover their retreat.

A breathless shout from within the line of knights, "Whenever you're ready, Dave! We're all just about knackered here." This prompted the next move, and Dave shouted the order.

"Do that push back drill and disengage. Make best speed back to the vehicles while we cover you."

A few more hacks and thrusts later, a shout came from one of them and they linked their shields and on another shouted countdown from one of them, gave a hard shove against the zombies still trying to climb over the wall of corpses. As they tumbled back down the gory slope of death, they knocked more over creating a gap and giving them the time to turn around and run back to the vehicles.

The timing and execution of the drill was so efficient that there was no need for any of us tracking backwards protecting the running knights to fire our weapons.

Within a few minutes, ramps were raised, doors were closed, and the convoy of forty-two people and one dog slowly moved off the cricket pitch and continued the journey.

CHAPTER EIGHTEEN

Retracing our route out of the village, I was puzzled when passing the end of Louise's parents' road, she told us that Shawn was stopping.

As soon as he had, Shawn leapt from the cab and carrying his weapon, ran up the road towards their house.

"Louise, what's he up to?" I asked.

"Tom, I don't know. He just told me to tell you we were stopping and then he ran off."

We could do nothing but wait, our eyes scanning everywhere for approaching zombies. It seemed longer, but it was only a few minutes before he returned, running at full speed, his weapon in one hand and objects held in his other. When he was closer, I could see what they were. He had gone to Louise's parents' house and gathered some picture frames. Thoughtfully getting her what were probably family photos to help her remember her sister, mother and father.

"Bugger me," I said, "he must in bloody love, the daft git. He's getting gifts for her now."

Everyone in my car laughed. I wasn't annoyed with him, he'd only put himself at risk and hadn't asked for any help from others.

It had only taken him a few minutes, so he hadn't delayed us at all.

We laughed as we all agreed that though the women would treat it as a very noble and gallant act, it would not stop the rest of us taking the piss out of him mercilessly.

I couldn't see from our position, but I could imagine Louise being very happy at what he had done.

A minute later he pulled away and we followed his lead back to the motorway. Dave sat beside me, refilling his empty magazines from a large can of loose bullets Chet had dragged over from the rear of the car. As I drove, I handed him mine that I'd dropped down my shirt when exchanging them for full ones grabbed from the pouches on the tactical vest I was wearing.

He was exuberant. Full of praise for the way the knights had virtually handled the situation by themselves. Hundreds had been terminated for the expenditure of very little ammunition. Every thrust, stab or hack from one of the many weapons the knights had at their disposal that killed one was a bullet saved as far as he was concerned.

Feeding bullets into the magazines, he described how as soon as he could, now that he had seen how truly effective medieval weaponry could be, he needed all of us to get trained to a greater or lesser extent in all aspects of the ancient weapons.

We could potentially field at least three times as many 'knights' into battle as we currently had, if we counted everyone including children above twelve, and that prospect got the Marine Sergeant very excited.

To raise his mood even more, I reminded him how effective crossbows could be. Shawn, when he'd fired his at the start of our adventure on Bodmin Moor, had killed zombies easily from a distance. I knew we had at least thirty different sorts of crossbows from the knights and a good quantity of bolts. And extra bolts could, with a little trial and error, be made from materials we could scavenge.

Becky's voice over the radio stopped his rhetoric.

"We need to find a place to stop soon. Everyone's exhausted, especially the knights. The children have been cooped up all day in the trailer and after fighting two battles today and losing poor Daniel, I don't think we can go on much longer, either physically or emotionally. I know you men think you're all big and tough, but I can see the state of everyone in the trailer and if we have to fight again without getting any rest, it might not go as well next time."

I looked at Dave. "What you think, mate?" I asked.

"Can't argue with her, pal. It *has* been non-stop all day and to be fair, I'm feeling pretty whacked, and we're trained to cope with long periods of stress. I have to keep reminding myself that I'm dealing with civvies now, too. And not just civvies, but children and babies as well." He smiled.

"I'll pull her up on her sexism, though. The women today fought just as hard as the men, so if she was implying that the women can last longer than men in combat situations, I will have to defend the honour of us boys."

"Good luck with that," I replied with raised eyebrows.

The demographics of our group meant we had more men than women, but that didn't mean the men did all the work. Everyone did, and could, shoot a gun and wield a zombie spear. Just now at the Village Hall, just as many women as men had stepped from the vehicles to protect the vicar when he performed his service and then joined the Marines to protect the knights' flanks as they fought the pack of zombies.

Dave picked up the radio.

"I agree. It's too late to try to reach Worcester and Steve's family. Shawn, Louise, since you're in the lead and have the best view, can you keep an eye out for a good place to stop? I don't need to tell you what to look for."

Louise confirmed that they understood and were both on the lookout.

Soon Louise broadcast that she knew of a farm that was coming up on the left. It was about half a mile off the main road and if it wasn't overrun, it would be a good place to stop for the night.

The farm looked a good choice, I decided, as the convoy pulled into its yard after driving up a long single-track drive. As the last vehicle in the convoy, we'd stopped and closed the gate just off the main road. It wouldn't stop a horde, but it would deter any from heading our way. If we had to leave in a hurry, any of our vehicles would easily be able to smash through it.

The farm was arranged in a typical layout. A large central courtyard that could easily accommodate all our vehicles was surrounded by a few farm buildings with the main farmhouse at one end. Walls and gates filled in the gaps between these buildings. The walls weren't high enough and the gates not strong enough to offer complete security, but they were better than nothing and would offer us a certain amount of protection, and they would delay any approaching zombies.

From much practice, we formed the square of vehicles quickly and one by one, the engines were turned off.

I could see two cars parked neatly in the yard, in front of the building I assumed was the farm shop I'd seen signs advertising on the main road. One was a small two-door compact and one was a larger estate car.

Dave called out to everyone, reminding them to stay put until he'd done the usual security sweep.

Grabbing our weapons, Chet and I joined him as we climbed down the ladder from the Volvo's roof. The outbuildings had open fronts, so we checked those first, and finding them empty, we moved on to the side of the yard that contained the farm shop. Passing the cars, I took a quick look inside them. Tapping Dave on the shoulder, I pointed at one of them.

A dog that looked to be dead lay in the luggage area of the estate car. A few of the windows on the car were opened for ventilation. All they did now though was let out the strong smell of faeces and decay.

"Poor mutt," I thought. Everyone knew the danger and stupidity of leaving dogs in cars in hot weather.

I looked at the doors to the shop. Maybe though, if you were just popping into somewhere for a second or two to pick something up, you'd consider it. The issue was, did a few moments turn into a lifetime for the owners of the car?

Dave indicated needlessly for us to be quiet and we approached the shop doors and looked inside. That solved the mystery of the dog.

Inside looked chaotic, shelves were knocked over and their contents scattered across the floor.

In the middle of the shop floor, three people were crouching over something on the floor. I could make out that two looked older and one was a young girl. I could not see what they were leaning over but I could imagine.

I looked at Dave and Chet, who nodded they were ready. I pushed the door open slowly and the three of us stepped in quietly. Chet's foot accidentally kicked against a can, which then rolled across the floor and clattered against some metal shelving.

Three heads lifted and began looking around for what had disturbed them. One of them, a lady who must have been in her seventies locked her eyes on us. She was holding a bone in her hands and her face and clothing were entirely covered with dried blood. Staring at us silently, she raised the bone to her mouth and continued gnawing upon it as she stood up. When they'd all raised themselves up, we could see what they were feeding on. A shoe, a few scraps of clothing and a pile of picked clean bones was all that was left of their victim. A lone white plastic clog the only indication it might have been someone who'd worked in the kitchen at the farm shop. They must have been feeding on their one victim for days, picking the corpse clean until there was nothing left.

"Clumsy bastard," chuckled Dave. "Oh well, they know we're here now. Let's get on with it."

He pulled a hand axe from the holder on his belt and stepped forward. We did the same. The axes had been one of the many items we had got from the farm supplies warehouse earlier. They all came with a holder that clipped to the belt and so made an ideal weapon for us to carry. Most of us had adopted them as our preferred primary close quarter weapon.

The axes easily smashed through skulls, their brains spilling across the floor as we withdrew them, adding another layer to the crusted and dried stains already covering it.

Our work was not yet done, we still had the main house to check. Holding the blood-dripping axes in our hands, we left the shop and trotted over to the front door of the farmhouse. The door was locked, but easily gave way to a well-aimed kick from Dave.

The house was a mess. The mess, though, told a story of a family's rapid, but organised departure. Wardrobes and chests of drawers were open in all the bedrooms and clothes that hadn't made it into bags had been left scattered everywhere. Food that hadn't been taken was still piled on the kitchen worktops. The large pantry next to the kitchen was empty. Most of the food left behind was perishable, showing that they'd had time to make choices about what to take. In the utility room a gun safe was open with the keys left in the lock, a lone gun was still in it and a few dropped cartridges littered the floor.

We would never know what happened to them. All I cared about was that the house they had left in such a hurry would provide us with an ideal shelter for the night.

Thirty minutes later, the smell of cooking from the kitchen grabbed our interest. Jim had gone to the farm shop and ignoring the carnage on the floor, had collected a lot of almost fresh vegetables and dried meat from the deli counter and after telling Maud to stop interfering with his creative genius, was making a huge pot of delicious smelling what he called in his own words, 'mush'.

While he was cooking, we had closed and reinforced the gates to the courtyard and arranged the vehicles to form a barrier around the front door, and a few of us spent some time securing the house. Scavenging some materials from the sheds on the property, we boarded up every ground floor window and door, except for the front door.

Some good news was that the dog in the car wasn't dead, as I had first thought; Daisy, after hearing about it, had insisted on going to check on it. And lucky she did.

As soon as she peered through the window of the car, she'd seen its chest barely rising and falling; her scream for help caused many of us to run over, weapons at the ready.

The dog, a German Shepherd who was probably less than a year old, was just hanging on to its last threads of life. Daisy had opened the back door of the car and had climbed in by the time I got there and was cradling the dog's head in her lap.

The car stank of dog faeces and urine and was scattered with ripped open food packages and remnants of plastic bags.

The dog most likely belonged to the old couple, or to the young girl who I imagined was their granddaughter, who had been feeding on the unfortunate shopworker until we intervened. They'd probably left the dog in the car with the rest of their shopping while they'd popped into the farm shop for something, and one or all of them had succumbed to the virus and turned while they were in there.

All speculation, but that was all there was to go on.

What had saved the dog was the shady spot where they'd parked the car and the fact that the car contained what probably had been their weekly shopping. It had kept it going until it had eaten the lot. Even though the car was in the shade for most of the day, the hot weather would still have made its interior incredibly hot. The heat and the lack of water had slowly been killing the dog until we arrived.

I carefully picked the dog up and with Daisy stroking its head, carried it into the house. Laying it on the floor in the lounge I handed it over to the care of Daisy and, under the guidance of some grown-ups, a whole troop of young nursing staff.

With the place secure and with only a small perimeter to watch and many hands to do it, everyone found themselves with some time on their hands and took the opportunity to relax and sit down. With so many of us, it was lucky that the house was large. Space was at a premium, but there was enough of it for everyone to sit down either around the large kitchen table or in one of the downstairs rooms, on a chair, table or sofa or on the carpet leaning against a wall.

Most of us kept checking in on the progress of the dog. It was a she, and Daisy had named her Princess. She was improving and after having water initially spooned into her mouth, was recovering well. She had not yet regained the strength to stand but was now able was drink from a bowl placed beside her.

The children were taking the warning seriously about not overcrowding her and respecting the fact that she had been through a traumatic period, and therefore her behaviour might be unpredictable. Princess lay there, though, looking at everyone around her, wagging her tail, proving she was on the mend and probably had a nice temperament.

Horace had been to see her and seemed very happy about the addition of what he probably considered to be a young and very attractive lady to the group.

We joked that he was now spending an equal amount of time begging for food from the kitchen and visiting his new love interest, no doubt telling her what a brave and heroic zombie fighter he was, and for her own safety she needed to stick as close to him as possible.

Once all the food had been eaten and Jim thanked profusely for singlehandedly producing a delicious meal to feed all of us, the children were ushered upstairs to bed.

They were delighted that Princess found the strength to follow them upstairs where once she was lifted onto the bed Daisy was sharing top to toe with the other children, she fell immediately asleep.

When I went upstairs to check on them ten minutes later, they were all sound asleep. Looking around the room, I sighed with acceptance at the new world we were now living in. The .22 rifles most of them had laid claim to and had proved their competence with during the day, were leaning against the wall. I picked one up to check it. The magazine was full, but the rifle, as had all the others leant against the wall, had its bolt pulled back and did not have a bullet chambered. In other words, they were in about as safe a condition that a loaded bolt-action rifle could be kept.

'Well done, them,' I thought, my trust in them growing.

Leaning over to adjust the blanket around Daisy, I saw she had placed the knife Shawn had given her at the very beginning on the bedside table next to her. Close to hand and ready to use.

Bending to kiss her forehead, a grunt from the middle of the bed got my attention. Princess was watching me through one eye. I looked at her and ruffled her ears. Her tail gave a few wags of appreciation before she lowered her head and closed her eyes again. She'd told me she knew I was there and watching me.

"Oh well," I thought, *"It looks as if the kids have got themselves another bodyguard and looking at the size of her paws, Princess is going to end up a very large one at that."* The smell, though, told me that she needed a bath in the morning.

Back downstairs the stresses of the past days were showing on everyone. A few bottles had been opened and passed around. I sat next to Becky, put my arm around her and took a sip of the wine I'd helped myself to.

The conversation was muted, no one really having the energy to liven things up.

I found my eyes drooping until Simon speaking up got my attention.

"Right then, folks. By my reckoning, this house has six other bedrooms, five doubles and a single. Now do not expect me to make a habit of this, but I think we should offer the couples in our group the chance to spend the night together. Alone.

The rest of us can easily keep watch, so go on, you lot, get yourselves to bed. And I do not want to hear one word of protest or we might all change our minds. And don't worry about Sarah, she'll be well looked after."

There was a general murmuring of agreement from all the others in the room.

I was going to protest as a matter of course, but Becky stood up and taking hold of my hand, said, "Thank you, Simon."

The three other couples all stood, thanked everyone and started to shuffle from the room.

I did the maths the same time as the others. There were two more bedrooms to fill.

Simon chuckled as he knew we'd worked it out.

"Maud. The single bedroom is for you, it's at the top of the stairs. If you don't use it, I will order Jim here to carry you up and keep guard outside your door all night, if that's what it takes for you to get a good night's sleep."

He then turned to Louise.

"The other one is for you, my dear. I'm so sorry for what you've had to go through today and nothing I can do will make up for that. I'm not sure if you want to spend the night alone or with someone, but the room is there for you."

Louise walked up to Simon and kissed him on the cheek, saying, "Thank you."

She then turned and took Shawn by the hand and silently led the shocked looking man upstairs.

The look that Maud gave the room stopped any comment before it could reach any lips.

Once they had left, Maud thanked Simon for his thoughtfulness and the couples trooped upstairs.

When I'd shut the door, I heard Ian say, "Friends! My arse. Shawn is one lucky git."

Trying not to laugh myself, Becky and I cuddled up in bed and despite what others thought we might be getting up to, we were both asleep within minutes.

Forty-two people and now two dogs quietly spend the night, thankful to have survived another day.

CHAPTER NINETEEN

Early the next morning the first movements around the house slowly roused everyone else and we all gathered downstairs in singles and groups.

Shawn wore a continually embarrassed look on his face and kept avoiding everyone's eye. He purposely didn't stand near any of his friends, as he clearly didn't want to be quizzed about last night's goings on.

He tried to go outside, claiming he wanted to check on the vehicles and do any repairs necessary before they left, and failed. when to a man, all his friends immediately jumped up and said they would help and followed him straight out of the door.

The women were far subtler with Louise, who was looking a lot happier today than she had been yesterday. Understandable, as yesterday she'd had to say goodbye to her parents. I decided to bide my time and listen to the exaggerated stories from his friends and later find out the truth from Becky.

Decisions needed to be made as two options had been put forward concerning the plan for the day.

The first option was to load up and carry on with our mission, initially to see if any of Steve's family had survived, a likelihood even he now admitted was remote, and then continue towards Warwick.

Becky was proposing the second option; that as we had found a reasonably secure and remote location and we'd all been operating for many days now under continuous and considerable duress and stress, even though we'd been doing exceptionally well, there was only so much we could take before mistakes started being made.

She did acknowledge, though, the need to fulfil our promise to Steve and his family, and that her proposal might go against that, but she was convinced that the safety of all of us relied on us being 'on top of our game' and that a day of rest and recovery would go a long way in ensuring our continued success.

No doubt what she was saying made sense, because we'd all been operating on adrenaline and instinct since it began. There had been a few periods where we'd been able to rest, mainly at Willie's farm and the Church, but those days had still been filled with frenetic activity and continual exertion, only interspersed with the occasional downtime.

The saying 'tired to the bone' would probably have been a good description of how we were feeling.

No one wanted to let Steve down and despite going against what everyone really felt, the consensus was that we must leave as soon as possible and get to Worcester.

Steve stood up and settled the discussion.

"Look, folks, I really appreciate what you're saying, but in all honesty, I think it will all be a waste of time. The odds of my family making it when we have not seen, apart from us, any other survivors, are not worth a bet. Don't get me wrong, I do want to check, as we did with Louise. Also, probably if I have to admit it, I'm a little afraid of what I might discover."

He looked upset for a moment, but soon got his emotions under control.

"Anyway, if they have survived, they will be at home. My mom was a hoarder and always kept cupboards full of food 'just in case'. And my dad's a DIY nut. The garage is always full of enough stuff to board up and secure the place up completely. If they have survived and are at home, we could turn up a week from now and they would still be there. What I suppose I'm trying to say is that another day won't make a difference. If they are at home and hunkered down, they will still be there tomorrow, so if everyone feels as knackered as I do, a make and mend day will do us the world of good."

No one was going to disagree with him, so the rest day option was gratefully accepted by us all.

When we weren't on lookout duty, which involved sitting in a chair at an upstairs window, we passed the day either doing light chores, resting, chatting or just dozing quietly on a bed or a spare bit of floor space.

The house still had water coming from the taps, maybe because it was supplied from its own source or the local mains system was gravity fed and still operated. Princess smelt no better and the children were tasked with giving her a bath.

Princess' recovery was remarkable. She was still a little unsteady on her feet and chose to lie down more than she stood, but she was a far cry from the starved, dehydrated close-to-death dog we'd found yesterday.

She even seemed to enjoy the bath that the children gave her. The adults not so much as she predictably escaped before being dried properly and chose the spot in the middle of the lounge that would hit the most of us when she shook herself thoroughly. Of course, we all dived everywhere, laughing and shouting in annoyance at the same time as trying to escape from what seemed like gallons of unwanted water spraying from her fur.

The children then decided to give Horace a bath. Strangely though, as soon as he saw what was happening to Princess, he disappeared. Only after a thorough hunt was he found hiding under a bed, where even the temptation of food would not make him budge to endure the what he obviously considered the torture and humiliation of getting washed.

He emerged only when he heard the water draining from the bath. He then cautiously stood next to Princess and kept one eye on her, as if concerned she might go into sudden and terminal shock from the obviously unhealthy bath she'd just had to endure, and one even more careful eye on anyone who approached him, just in case emptying the bath had been a cunning ruse and he was next.

Meanwhile, a few useful tasks, using many willing hands, were completed easily throughout the day.

Using hoses and brushes, the vehicles were cleaned of the worst of the blood that covered them and body parts that still clung to various places. No one knew how the zombie virus really spread apart from bites, and so we could only guess that it most probably lived in the blood and tissues of the turned. Was it still active even when not attached to the host? Cleaning the vehicles of the worst made sense. A few of us then spent some time checking over the adaptations we'd made. Dents were banged out and a few improvements made to keep strengthening them.

Every fuel tank on the vehicles and empty Jerry can was filled from the red diesel tank in the yard.

The farmhouse was searched for anything useful. A lot had already been taken by the owners when they'd packed up and fled, but some things remained, hidden in the back of drawers and cupboards. Batteries, candles, matches and lighters, along with some carefully chosen kitchen utensils, were added to a pile we were creating to be loaded.

With so many of us now, it had become apparent that we could do with more 'camping items' to make us more comfortable. Most of the ones not in a comfy bed or on a sofa had spent the night sleeping on the floor, lying under the blankets or duvets we had brought with us. Bed rolls and sleeping bags would have made it a more comfortable experience.

They would also be a good idea to have going forwards. It was universally agreed that we needed to find a camping shop. If we found the right one, it would also have many more useful items for us to take.

The contents of the farm shop that were not perishable were retrieved and added to the pile, as well as some tools we found in some of the sheds. Any remaining clothing, footwear and bedding left in the house was sorted through and anything claimed or deemed useable by any of us was added to the pile too.

Dave and I inspected the shotgun that had been left in the gun safe. It was an old one, so I could see why he might have left it behind if the farmer had had choices to make. But it looked to be in serviceable condition and we added it to our impressive arsenal, along with the cartridges we scrabbled around the floor to pick up.

Shane chose to spend the day cleaning and servicing as many guns as he could. He was told not to, but he said it was how he used to relax before. He claimed a corner of the dining room floor and used his gunsmithing tools and a cleaning kit, whistling to himself happily as he disassembled, inspected, serviced and cleaned all our personal weapons and the others we'd stored in the vehicles.

Dave, even though we already had many thousands of shotgun cartridges, was grateful for every additional one we could find.

He had one he'd picked up from the floor in the farmhouse in his hand and held it up to us.

"One day this one cartridge might be all I have left between me and certain death by being eaten by one of those unholy bastards out there. We have the knights and we're all going to learn to fight like them, but until the ammunition runs out, which I think it *will* before we've got rid of every one of them out there, guns are going to be imperative to our survival too.

When we get to Warwick Castle, I don't care if we have rooms full of ammunition and guns. In my opinion, we're never going to have enough.

Once it's secure, we know that food should be easy to find. A couple of supermarket raids should give us enough to keep us going for a long time. Or we could even find a few of the abandoned food lorries we know are littering the roads everywhere, and drive them back to the castle.

"It's guns and ammunition that are going to be harder to find. I know we can raid the local gun shops and keep widening the search. But the weapons I really want won't be available from them. I keep having weird thoughts about this castle. When everyone else thinks of a castle, I imagine they picture one with cannons and guards with bows and arrows, throwing rocks and boiling tar down upon the besieging forces. I have a vision of it brimming with heavy weaponry. Machine guns positioned on the ramparts, mortars and artillery set up to rain death down upon any one who dares to attack."

He looked at me.

"Somehow, I think that however good the defences are, if a super-herd ever finds us, it won't be the walls, swords, pikes or axes that will save us. It will be lead and high explosives. And a lot of it, at that. It's how we get hold of it that's the problem. We're going to have to go on some serious scavenging missions to make me happy."

He slipped the cartridge he was carrying into his top pocket and smiled at me.

"Tom, I'll keep that cartridge there, I think. Because if I find myself reaching for it, you can pretty much guarantee we're fucked."

I clapped him on the back.

"As long as you don't say 'I told you so' when you do. Dave, I agree with you. As soon as we're secure at Warwick Castle, and I hope it will be soon, then its defence is going to be top of my agenda. If you can get hold of some heavy stuff, you won't be getting any complaints from me, or anyone else for that matter."

Becky was right, a day away from the continuous travelling and fighting to survive was what we needed. It was a luxury, but a luxury we were lucky enough to be able to take. Not that any of us could truly relax. After all, a swarm of undead zombies could appear at the walls of our temporary sanctuary at any moment.

The opportunity, though, to sit and have nothing to do but drink a cup of tea and chat with others in the group was a tonic we all appreciated.

I could feel my batteries slowly recharging as the day wore on between occasional guard duty, completing a few lightweight tasks, and resting.

The children were allowed, under strict instructions about not making too much noise, to play in the yard. Princess, getting stronger by the hour, enjoyed retrieving the ball they kept throwing for her.

Weapons over our shoulders, most of us drifted outside to watch over the children.

Sarah was laid on a rug outside and she enjoyed kicking her legs and playing with some toys in the late afternoon sun. We all smiled at her attempts to start crawling that continually ended in her flopping back down on her belly, her arms and legs moving uncoordinatedly when for a split second it looked as if she was going to manage it, the wise sages amongst us predicting it would not be long.

I just hoped it happened when we were safe and secure at our destination.

We laughed at Horace. He kept trying to chase the ball, but the young legs of Princess were just too fast for him. Eventually, to save his embarrassment, he gave up and went to lie down next to Sarah, who squealed with delight at the big, furry, moving teddy bear with a wet tongue that tickled. Horace let her use him for a climbing frame; lying there, tail wagging, ignoring her poking fingers as they explored his nose and ears and eyes. A complete contrast to the snarling, growling, barking beast of a dog who had fought zombies the day before, biting and attacking any that got too close.

Another benefit of the day was that the volunteer cooks had time to prepare a delicious feast for our evening meal. A few of the chickens that free ranged around the farm were caught and dispatched. Then, using the commercial size ovens in the farm shop, which still worked thanks to the farm's own gas supply, they cooked a fantastic roast chicken dinner.

As they finished preparing it, a team of us carried out some tables and chairs from the restaurant section of the farm shop and set them up in the courtyard. The restaurant was unfortunately open plan and connected to the shop, leaving on display the carnage that was too big to cover up. Therefore, if we wanted to eat together, al fresco was the only option.

At the end of a delicious meal and before forty-two people and two dogs headed off for an early night, the group graciously allowed the ones who had used the bedrooms the previous night the same privilege, so we could use every hour of daylight the following day. The happy realisation was also reached that no one needed to do the washing up.

CHAPTER TWENTY

Up and alert before daybreak, hushed groups, trying to let the sleeping children have as long as possible in bed before waking them, finished the final loading of the vehicles.

The sun was just lightening the eastern sky as we started the engines and followed Shawn in convoy down the drive. I stopped for a minute when we reached the main road to allow Dave to climb down from the car and close the gate, before turning left and heading back to the motorway and Worcester. We'd chosen to go to another junction further up the motorway. The road from Louise's parents' village went past both junctions and as we'd seen smoke ahead on the carriageway when we'd left the motorway a few days before, we thought it might circumvent whatever problem may or may not lie ahead.

Bringing up the rear, I was drinking from a travel cup filled with coffee Becky handed me after I'd carried the sleepy children downstairs and into the trailer.

Jamie had taken the fourth space in my car after volunteering the day before. After he'd practised getting in and out a few times, using the ladder while wearing his armour, we agreed to him joining us. It wasn't easy for him, climbing up the ladder wearing his armour, but he could manage it and if it didn't work out, we could always try another volunteer. He'd chosen not to pick up one of the spears, saying that now he was out of the trailer and lower to the ground, he would stick with his axe. In my mirror, Jamie standing on the rear seat of my car was a sight I didn't think I would get used to for a long time. Wearing his armour and helmet, he stood with his axe resting on his shoulder. The wind caused by the speed I was driving ruffled his long beard. In another age and if the car was substituted by a Viking longboat, he would have made the perfect image of a Viking, ready for battle, standing in the prow of his boat, preparing to leap ashore to keep up the Viking tradition of rape and pillage.

It was a beautiful morning as the slowly rising sun lit up more of the countryside we were driving through. All my passengers were standing up on the seats, not for any reason apart from to enjoy the view. Soon, though, we would be heading into what we considered more unknown territory.

The information we'd received from the soldiers only covered the motorway as far as Cheltenham. It could be clear or blocked, and there might even be another roadblock put in place by some local hooligans. We just didn't know what to expect.

Nothing we hadn't handled before, so the level of concern amongst the group wasn't really any higher than it had been previously. But there was no such thing as relaxing when travelling through a countryside where the entire population was flesh eating zombies whose only goal was to eat you.

I also felt more comfortable, as the further north we went, the closer we got to areas I knew better. If diversions needed to be made, I would be more familiar with the roads, and possibly more familiar too with the best way the navigate around them. Maps did not show everything, and nothing could ever beat local knowledge.

Shawn slowed down as we approached the motorway slip road and instead of driving down it, he continued straight and chose to drive onto the raised bridge that overlooked it, and there he stopped.

Halting in a line behind him, we all had a good view of the road we'd planned to take.

As far as I could see, both carriageways were a scrapheap of unrecognisable twisted, burnt and still smoking metal. Whatever had happened had been catastrophic and massive and it answered the question that had arisen when we'd seen the smoke rising ahead when leaving the motorway at the junction before this to reach Louise's parents' village.

The soldiers would have joined the motorway at the same junction we'd left it at, so they probably wouldn't have noticed it.

There was no point dwelling on it, though. The way we intended to go was impassable and there was nothing we could do to change that.

Louise's voice came over the radio, "Alternative route B, the A38 is straight ahead. Shawn's just checking his map."

I smiled to myself. Anyone who lived in Birmingham was familiar with the A38. It was one of the main arterial roads that led out of the south and the north of the city. Heading south, it was called the Bristol Road. Quite simply because it went to Bristol; the city we'd found Shawn's friends alive and well in. Until the M5 motorway was built it was the main route for anyone from Birmingham to take to head to the southwest of the country.

My grandad, who died many years ago, never took the M5 when he went on his annual holiday to Weston-super-Mare. He never quite trusted the motorway that had replaced it and always refused to use it.

"Well, maybe he was right," I thought, thinking fondly of the old man I hadn't thought about for years.

The A38 mainly ran parallel to the M5, but it did pass through a lot of towns and villages, making the route potentially more hazardous. But then again, what other choice did we have? Shawn would know this too, and would divert back to the motorway as soon as possible.

Shawn revved his engine, and the convoy headed off again.

Dave sat down and studied the map.

"Nothing we haven't done before, mate. Just stick close to the one in front and let us do the rest."

"Piece of cake, matey."

Louise's warning of "zombies ahead" made Dave put the map down and pick up a spear.

I listened carefully to Louise's instructions as she called out course changes for the rest of us to follow. Bringing up the rear, there wasn't much left for us by the time the other vehicles had speared, smashed or driven over anything that was ahead.

If one was left standing, the passengers in my car did their best to add it to the tally for the day. Dave had to tell Jamie to calm it down a bit when he, in excitement at how successful his axe proved, lifted himself out of the car and was sitting astride the roof with one leg in the car and one leg out, swinging his axe like a polo player at any Zombie within reach. Dave's point was proved when Chet had to grab onto his belt when an overenthusiastic swing that took the head clean off a passing one caused him to overbalance and almost fall out. Chet yanked him back in the car, where he ended up upside down on the seat with his feet sticking through the roof.

He and Chet became helpless with laughter as he tried to right himself. His chainmail had ridden up around his waist and arms, rendering him completely immobile. It took ten minutes for both Dave, who was trying not to see the funny side, and Chet, pushing and pulling him to get him the right way around and back on his feet.

Jamie took the bollocking Dave dished out to him, knowing he'd put himself and others at risk by his actions.

Miles slipped away as any blockage we found was easily dealt with by Shawn and although we encountered a few concentrations of zombies, mainly in the towns and villages we passed, we didn't have to slow our pace as we sliced through them. Shawn led us back to the motorway two junctions further up and we continued north.

Approaching the next junction, I saw a sign advertising a retail estate that was located near the junction. A well-known sports shop that sold everything from tents to ski gear and canoes to bikes was advertising its presence on the sign listing all the businesses located there. I picked up the radio.

"Hey, guys," I broadcast. "Shall we try and get the camping gear we're after? We can see the buildings from here and it looks to be one of those large out-of-town sites. If it's too dangerous, there should be plenty of room to just turn around and continue back up the motorway."

All calls came back agreeing it was at least worth a look and we followed Shawn as he drove up the slipway and entered the retail park, the entrance of which was right off the motorway is-land itself.

I breathed a sigh of relief as we entered the vast parking area. Again, the apocalypse had hit before trading had begun. There were a few cars parked and one or two zombies stumbling around, but compared to what we had experienced before, the place was as good as empty.

Shawn drove straight to the front of the shop we wanted. Its shutters were closed, apart from one which protected a small door. The door was open, but nothing was in sight.

Dave picked up the radio and began issuing instructions, get-ting everyone into the correct position.

The few zombies that were present had predictably started heading in our direction, so Dave asked a few of the knights on the bus to deal with them before we entered the shop.

While they were being dealt with, the assault squad, as we had begun calling them, stepped from the bus and walked down the ramp on the trailer to gather together.

A few of us helped to lift the ramp back onto the trailer so we could close the rear door and protect its remaining occu-pants.

When the knights returned from killing the zombies, we began discussing entering the shop. We knew that it was going to be huge inside, with many aisles and other rooms that needed to be checked before we could call it safe.

We decided to commit most of our people to the operation. The ones outside would remain in their vehicles and if any more zombies appeared, they could easily contact us using the radios and we'd be close enough to easily exit the building and support them if we were needed.

The plan was for us to enter the building and stay together as one large group until we were satisfied it was safe. Then we would split into smaller groups, each tasked with gathering items from a list we were hastily drawing up.

"Ok, everyone," Dave called to us all, "my boys will lead the way with half the knights backing them up. If the rest of the knights can bring up the rear watching our backs, that would be great. Remember, if it goes to shit in there, stay together and we will exit as one unit. If this place is like others I've been to, it will be a maze of aisles, so don't panic. It will be nothing we haven't done before, just in a tighter space, that's all. I want everyone to stay sharp. If we get attacked, only the ones facing them directly will be able to fight, limiting how many we can kill. Do not separate yourselves from the group, thinking you can help by getting around their back. It will divide our forces and could get us more in the shit."

I knew what he was doing. We had had such success with the tactics we had created that overconfidence and complacency could creep into our thinking. He was trying to stop that before it got one or more of us killed.

With faces looking a bit more serious, we checked our own and each other's gear, made sure our weapons were loaded and easily to hand, and we prepared to enter the building.

The light coming through the clear panels in the roof provided enough to see by as we walked through the door and gathered inside.

Some displays were knocked over and bloodstains marked the floor, indicating that something had gone on.

Tension built, as gripping our weapons tighter, we worked our way further into the building, our ears straining to try and catch the slightest sound.

Dave, who was in the lead group, raised his fist in the air as he approached the end of the aisle we were cautiously walking down, and we all stopped.

Quickly peering around the corner ahead, he held his fist high in the air and pointed with a finger to the left. He was clearly indicating something was ahead. He gave the universal forwards sign and we all followed him around the corner.

The end of the aisle opened into a larger area that used to display tents. Most of these were knocked flat by the throng of zombies that were all standing with their backs to us, crowding around some high racking.

Three people wearing the uniform of the shop were lying, sprawled, on the top shelves of the racks.

Quietly, Dave indicated for some of us to spread out to form a line, and using hand signals, he pointed at others to keep watching our backs.

Standing in the line I counted twenty zombies. My trepidation dropped, we had handled this many before, just not in such an enclosed environment.

The ones on the rack had not noticed us. They hadn't even moved. It was hard to tell if they were dead or alive. If they had been up there since the start, then the chances were they would have died from dehydration or starvation. But if they were dead, wouldn't the zombies have lost interest in them?

Dave called out softly, "Ready, everyone?" and kicked the rack next to him. A dull sound reverberated around the deathly quiet shop.

As one, the zombies slowly turned and faced us. They too, apart from a few in normal clothes, were dressed in the shop's uniform. Movement on the rack caught my attention as two of the people on the top rack weakly raised their heads. One slowly raised his arm and held it up. He opened his mouth, but no words came out. He looked to be in a very poor state.

The need for quiet was now over, we had the attention of the undead and they were slowly staggering towards us.

Dave shouted, "Knights, form a line and deal with them. We'll watch your backs."

Jamie spoke first. From what they had told me, that meant he was now in command.

"Shields and hand weapons, lads."

It took a few moments for them to form up and link their shields into a solid barrier before stepping forward to attack. Their skill, technique and discipline were such that even before they swung their first blow, I knew it was over. Within minutes, all the zombies were on the floor, blood and brains spilling from the wounds caused by their deadly weapons.

They then checked each one was dead. The ones with swords thrust them through eye sockets or mouths if they were in any doubt.

"Great work once again, lads," said Dave.

We all looked up at the racking. Two of the three were trying to raise themselves up. You didn't need to be an expert to see they were in a terrible state. Their filthy, emaciated faces made them look more dead than alive. The third lay ominously still and unmoving. It was clear they were in no condition to help themselves, and we needed to climb up and help them.

Dave spread the rest of us out in a cordon while he and Shawn put their weapons down and climbed up the racking.

"We need to get them down now," he shouted a short time later. "One is dead and the other two are barely hanging on."

Our mission to gather supplies had inadvertently changed into a rescue mission. The three must have been on top of the racking since the beginning. Escaping from their work colleagues and unable to go anywhere, they had been stuck there.

I looked up. For them to have survived, they must have been able to get hold of something to sustain them, otherwise they would have died of dehydration long ago.

Hopefully if they recovered, we would find out their story, but for now the priority was to get them down and start looking after them the best we could.

Dave called down, "Can someone get some rope? I think the best way to get them down will be to tie a rope around them and lower them down."

I pointed to the knight near me.

"Come on, lads, follow me. There must be some ropes in the climbing section. Let's go and find it."

With the knights acting as my guards, I cautiously walked through the shop, all the while checking for any stragglers lurking and waiting for the chance to sink their teeth into living flesh.

Luckily finding the aisles deserted, I found the climbing section of the shop. The shelves and racks were filled with all the paraphernalia a climber needed to pursue the sport. Grabbing a few bundles of ropes that were hanging from a hook, we hurried back to the others Dave and Shawn had assisted the two who were still alive into a seating position and were helping them drink from a canteen. The water was already improving their condition and their movements looked more coordinated. When Dave signalled, I threw the ropes up to him.

He wasted no time unravelling the rope and tying a loop around the first one's chest, under his arms. With Dave taking the strain, the young man weakly shuffled to the edge and tried to climb down. His strength gave way and he would have fallen, but Dave, anticipating this, had a tight hold on the rope and slowly feeding it through his hands, gently lowered him into the outstretched arms of the ones waiting below, who grabbed him and lowered him to the ground. Some began helping him, while the others stood ready to help Shawn as he began lowering down the young woman he was attending to.

Gathering around as they lay on the floor, we could see how close to death they still were.

"Let's get them out of here," said Dave. "They're going to need some careful looking after if they're going to recover. It's not just a case of giving them food and water. They look so far gone they could be in danger of organ failure if we don't get it right."

Jim spoke up, "I had some training as part of a disaster relief programme once. We got told how to treat famine victims before medical help arrived."

"Great, Jim," replied Dave. "I would say these two fall into that category. You're their doctor now. If a few of you could help carry them outside, you can begin nursing them back to health.

The rest of us need to check this whole place is clear and then we need to start shopping."

We made some stretchers out of some sturdy signs, and the boys were carried outside and placed into the trailer, where Jim began supervising their care.

Twenty minutes later we were satisfied that no surprises waited for us in any of the many back rooms the store had, and we began what we had intended to do and gathered more supplies.

There were so many items for us to choose from, all of which we could put to good use, and it was difficult not to empty the whole shop. We did know that we could always raid similar shops in the future, so there was no point being daft, and we only took items from the list we had hastily agreed between ourselves.

But the van and the bus still got filled up with sleeping bags, tents, clothing, torches and many other items we just had to take. I did resist the temptation to take one of the canoes I'd always decided I absolutely needed whenever I had visited one of the chain's shops before.

The two patients were responding to their treatment. When I checked on them between pushing fully loaded trollies from the store, Jim was carefully assisting them to take small sips from an energy drink. He told me they were doing okay and asked if one of us could get some clothes for them from the store, so they could change them out of their filth-encrusted clothes, which were a health hazard.

When we had everything we needed, we all boarded our vehicles and continued the journey north.

Steve took over Jim's place on Simon's Land Rover. We were now forty-four and two dogs.

CHAPTER TWENTY-ONE

Glancing left as we drove over a bridge that crossed the River Avon, I slowed down, sure I'd seen a boat emerging from under the bridge as we passed over it.

I got Dave's attention, and he craned his neck to look back and confirmed he could see it too. None of the other vehicles ahead of me would have seen it, because it would have been under the bridge as they drove over it. By pure chance, I'd caught sight of it out of the corner of my eye.

Dave told the others to stop and I reversed back up the carriageway, stopping in the middle of the bridge.

"Cover me," was all he said as he grabbed his rifle and climbed down from the car, scrambled over the central barrier and ran to the railing at the side of the carriageway. Needing to answer the questions that were coming through the radio, I picked it up and told them what I'd seen, and that Dave was trying to contact them. I was questioned whether I wanted them to turn around and head back. In the time it had taken me to spot the boat, to slow down for Dave to confirm what I'd seen, and to get the others to stop, they had got a few hundred meters ahead of us. Then I'd reversed another hundred metres back along the bridge.

I told them not to bother yet. The motorway had been zombie free for a while.

Dave was shouting over the bridge. I couldn't make out what was being said, but he was having a conversation with them.

Eventually he pushed away from the side of the bridge and jogged back over to us.

"Tom, get the others back here to form square please. The boats are mooring and one or two of them are coming up to meet us. I told them I would start heading their way to escort them."

"Which side are they mooring?" I asked.

"I think they're dropping anchor in the middle of the river and using a small boat to reach the bank, if that helps. Why?"

"We're in the middle of a long bridge. Surely it would be better to form our square at the end where they'll be appearing," I said, a smile of 'oh what a good idea that is' playing across my face.

"Smart arse," he replied. "Okay I'll give you that. Just let me go and look."

He hopped back over the central barrier and looked down at the river, turned and jogged back to us and pointed towards where the others were waiting.

"That way. I'll get the others to start getting into position." Simon picked up the radio as I drove towards them.

Before we got there, he turned to Chet and Jamie.

"Can you two come with me please? We'll jump out when they're getting into position and we'll go to meet them."

Shawn had moved forward the short distance to the end of the bridge and by the time I turned up, the others were getting themselves into position around him. Stopping to let my three passengers out, I watched them run to the barrier, climb over it and disappear from view before pulling into the final position in the square.

The news that we were going to meet more survivors had got everyone excited. As soon as the ramp was lowered and doors opened, we gathered in the middle of the square and waited eagerly for them to arrive.

Daisy kept Princess on a lead when she brought her down from the trailer. The last thing any of us wanted was for her to run off, requiring us to chase her. Horace could be trusted and was never far from Ian, anyone with food, or the children. She was well behaved, though, and didn't pull on the lead and was happy to follow Daisy. An indication her previous owners had trained her well.

Jim stayed in the trailer to continue caring for our two new arrivals.

Today had gone well so far, apart from the diversion, which hadn't slowed us down much, and the visit to the retail park. We were about halfway to Worcester by my estimate. It had only taken us about three hours so far and it wasn't ten o'clock in the morning yet. I didn't know how long we were going to spend with these people we were just about to meet, but when we continued, and if we encountered no more problems, we should be ready to try to enter Worcester an hour after we started moving again.

All heads turned to watch Dave and the others climb over the barrier and walk towards us. The two strangers stopped briefly and stared with obvious amazement at our eclectic mix of vehicles, before following them and squeezing through the gap we'd left in our wall of vehicles.

I welcomed them and introduced myself before asking them what we all wanted to know: their story.

Their names were Graham and Arthur. After gratefully accepting some tea we poured from a thermos flask, they began.

Not knowing each other before the virus hit, they were both holidaying on the River Severn with their families, when they woke up one morning at neighbouring moorings at an isolated spot on the River Severn near Shrewsbury, to hear the news that was broadcasting over the radio and television.

Confident it was an elaborate practical joke and being the social bunch that the boating community was, and neither party being in a rush to get to any destination, they were enjoying a coffee on Graham's boat while their children played on the river bank with new found friends. That was when the reality of the situation came crashing home after they spotted a body floating towards them, slowly being led to them on the lazy current.

Bursting into action, the two men hurriedly jumped into Graham's tender he towed behind his boat to retrieve the body, while their wives tried to call the emergency services. To their horror, the body, that of a young man, was dead and appeared to have terrible bite marks over his face and neck. They could tell that the injuries were fresh and had only happened recently.

Dragging the body onto the bank, they could do no more than to cover it with a blanket and wait for the emergency services to arrive. The problem was they couldn't contact anybody, and they knew enough that they shouldn't disturb a potential crime scene, but they were at a loss to know what to do next. Then more bodies began to appear from upstream, all showing wounds of some description.

Terrified of what they might find, but also knowing that they needed to know, they decided to leave the body where it was and investigate what was going on further up the river. Cautiously making their way towards Shrewsbury, they turned around before they got there. The normally calm and beautiful river had turned into a carnal house of terror. More and more bodies filled the river and even from a distance Shrewsbury looked to be completely ablaze. Both men were forced to take up positions in the bows of their boats and use boat hooks to push more and more bodies out of the way out of respect for them and also because they were fearful of fouling their propellers.

At a few points, roads ran next to the river, and there it was confirmed to them that the unbelievable news must have been telling the truth. Watching in disbelief, they saw cars tearing down the roads, the faster drivers completely disregarding their own safety as well as that of anyone else as they forced others off the road in their desperation to escape. Crashed cars that still contained living people were ignored.

Normal human nature was to help these poor people, but it was clear that normal was not the rule of the day. Unwilling to moor the boats on the banks of the river, they found a small island in the middle of the flow and tied up, spending the next hours watching the news reports in disbelief, until one by one they went off the air to be replaced by the looping message from the Government.

Indecision reigned between the two distraught families brought together by the horror of what was occurring right around them. They simply did not know what to do next, until the noise of an approaching boat made them run up onto the flybridge of Graham's Cruiser. Its engines were roaring as it blasted along on full power, rocking from side to side erratically as if out of control. It was heading straight towards them. Fearing it might crash straight into them, but not having the time to do anything about it, they scrambled to the sides of the boat and prepared to jump off onto the island when at the last moment, it veered away from them and crashed at full speed into the bank opposite. Its momentum hurled it up the bank, its bow crushed and mangled as it smashed through trees and shrubs, ending up mostly out of the water, its propellers still spinning at maximum revolutions, churning the water, with its engine screaming in protest.

Shaken up from the near miss, they looked across at what was left of the once sleek boat. Its driver lay crumpled and unmoving on the bridge, either dead or severely injured, they couldn't tell which. The news reports and radio broadcasts had shown and described the terrible happenings around the country, but that was in the third person, still not quite believable or real.

Graham was looking at the boat through his binoculars, looking for any movement from the driver, when more movement from the boat caught their attention. A passenger emerged from the cabin of the boat. Binoculars were not needed to see the person was a woman and she was alive, but seriously injured. She was covered in blood and was crawling along the deck, both her legs sticking out at unnatural angles from the knees, obviously badly broken. It looked to the watchers as if she was crawling towards her partner to check on his condition. Eventually she reached him.

Graham had the best view through his binoculars and it was when he threw them down and started retching, that they all knew that there was no denying it. A zombie apocalypse had started.

The woman was not rendering aid, she was eating him, ripping chucks of flesh from his body and devouring them.

In panic and the urgent need to get away from what they were witnessing, they untied the boats from the trees they'd moored them to and headed back downstream together. Eventually, after seeing more evidence of death and destruction on either bank as they passed close to roads and houses, and fearful of going near the banks at all, they moored at another island to get together again and plan what the hell to do next.

Logistically, they were both in good shape. As they were both at the start of their holidays, both boats had enough fuel for a few weeks' gentle river cruising and food to last for the same period. It was where to go and what to do that they had no idea about. The obvious answer, from what they had witnessed, was that the river seemed to be the safest place to be, the land beyond the banks too terrifying to contemplate setting foot on.

Setting up a watch rota so one of their group was always on lookout, they remained at their island sanctuary for days, supplementing their dwindling food supplies by fishing, and conserving fuel by cooking on a camp fire on the island. Constantly monitoring the radio channels, both marine and land-based for any news, they waited.

From their isolated position they didn't see another living soul. Bodies continually floated past, reminding them of what was happening, but they had no contact with anyone. Their first experience with a zombie was when the lookout on deck spotted what they thought was a live person hanging onto a floating log, weakly thrashing around trying to get their attention. Graham and Arthur immediately untied the tender and starting the small outboard motor, went to help.

What they found was a zombie who had somehow impaled itself on a large tree branch that was now floating downstream. Its eyes locked on them as they approached, it reached its arms out towards them, growling and snapping its teeth. Recoiling in horror, Graham just managed to engage reverse and avoid coming into contact with it. Keeping at a safe distance, they followed the log and its trapped monster, studying it carefully, again trying to comprehend that what they were seeing was real.

There was no way the person with the injuries it had could still be alive. Its throat was ripped out and half of its face was devoid of flesh. And it had a branch protruding through its chest, an injury that would alone have been enough to end its life.

When they had returned to the boats and told their families, the children, who had more zombie experience through video game and TV shows, instructed the adults on the best way they knew to kill zombies. Anything that could be used as a head smashing, brain-destroying weapon was found and placed ready to use.

One morning a few days ago they picked up a faint and barely audible broadcast on the marine emergency channel. Using their scant knowledge, they jury-rigged an extension to the antenna to see if they could pick up the faint and intermittent signal better.

It worked. The message was being relayed from another private craft further down the River Severn. Their equipment did not have the range to reply, but they listened avidly to the message.

The Royal Navy was sheltering in the Solent and all remaining Royal Navy ships worldwide were making best speed to their location. The message informed anyone listening to make their way to their location, if at all possible.

That galvanised them into action. Now they had a goal, something to stop them just sitting there waiting for something to happen. Both experienced boaters, they pulled out maps and charts and began plotting the course. Even though they spent most of their times on rivers, both boats were seaworthy enough to make the journey. The main issue would be fuel. Depending on sea and tide conditions, they would probably need to refill their tanks a few times and that worried them.

Normally when undertaking such a journey, you would have every safe harbour, anchorage and ports with fuel, water and other facilities mapped and planned. Access to some might be restricted due to tide times and conditions which might alter your choice, but you would always have a safe anchorage to moor your boat if you planned it correctly.

Now the tide times and conditions were the only known quantity. Sea conditions and weather, since the weather and shipping forecasts had stopped, would be unknown. It was impossible to know if any of the refuelling points were safe too.

The number of unknown factors meant danger. They both knew well enough the normal dangers any sea journey could entail. All the unknowns made the prospect a truly daunting one.

Pooling all their knowledge and experience, they reached the conclusion that the best course of action would be to procure enough fuel to render the need to touch land unnecessary. The food supplies could be stretched and if the weather and sea conditions turned against them, they could drop anchor in one of the numerous coves, bays, estuaries and inlets along the coast until conditions improved enough for them to continue. Finding enough fuel was the only problem they needed to solve, which is why we had spotted them.

Leaving their island sanctuary, they journeyed down the river, intending to try every wharf and boatyard along the route until they found a safe place to get the fuel they needed. Unfortunately, time and time again they found every location swarming with shambling herds of what they began calling Walkers, after *The Walking Dead* TV series.

Steve stopped them at this point, knowing they'd travelled through Worcester on their journey south, and asked them what they'd seen in the city. He explained that his family lived there and that we were going there to see if they were somehow, miraculously, still alive.

The news wasn't good. They hadn't even stopped to check the numerous boat yards and refuelling points they knew were there, because the whole river frontage was swarming with walkers, who as soon as they noticed them, headed towards them and blindly walked or fell off the raised embankments straight into the river in their hundreds. Most sank immediately but some, buoyed up by air trapped in their clothes, thrashed their way towards them.

Worcester was the first place they had to resort to killing them, using the sharp end of their boat hooks to stab down into the heads of the ones who managed to reach the sides of their boats.

Graham was apologetic to Steve when he described how the city looked to have been ravaged by fires, which they could still see burning in places.

Steve listened carefully to the report, trying to hide his emotions, and then he thanked him and asked him to continue their story.

By the time they reached Tewksbury, finding similar conditions at all possible places, they were getting very concerned if they would ever find anywhere safe enough to get the fuel they needed.

Running out of ideas, they chose to head up the River Avon, which merges with the Severn at Tewksbury, to see if that would yield better results.

Only this morning they found a boatyard not far upstream from where we were standing now, which was deserted of both the living and the dead. We'd spotted them as they were heading back to continue their journey, after filling their internal fuel tanks till they overflowed, and then deck-loading as many barrels and containers of extra fuel as they could without affecting the stability of their crafts too much. By their reckoning, if they maintained a slow, laborious but efficient speed, they should be able to make it.

We were now temporarily fifty-two and two dogs.

CHAPTER TWENTY-TWO

Graham and Arthur were both eager to hear our stories, but the news that the Royal Navy was still operational was greeted with both joy and pride by the Marines present, who insisted on asking questions that neither man could answer.

Once they'd calmed down, we gave them the short story of who we were, how we had met and where we were going and why. Short story it may have been, but so much had happened to us in that time that it still took a while to tell it. They were, naturally enough, full of questions about what we'd witnessed, and they were eager to learn anything they could about the zombies and our theories about how it spread. We answered their questions to the best of our ability, telling them what was guesswork and speculation, and the facts we actually knew.

It took Maud to break up the discussions by interrupting us all and saying,

"It is absolutely fantastic that we have met others. But, we're still going to end up departing in opposite directions. So, all of us standing around here chatting is not getting any of us any closer to where we want to be, is it?"

She turned to Graham and Arthur.

"What we should be asking you is what do you need and how can we help you. You've mentioned food. Do you need some? I'll get some of these big tough men here to ask you if you need any guns or anything, because I'm sure we can spare a few, but if you can have a think if there is anything else we can help you with, have a quick think now and let one of us know.

Also, your families must be going frantic with worry with you being gone for so long, so one of you should at least wave over the edge of the bridge at them."

Maud, as usual, had got it right. It was great to meet up with fellow survivors, especially as these were the first ones we had met who were not in a desperate situation and needing our help.

I placed my hand on her shoulder.

"And this is Maud, the true leader of our little group. As none of us is brave enough to go against her wishes, I think we should do as she suggests."

I held my arms open in an expansive gesture.

"What can we help you with? We have food to spare, and weapons and other equipment you might find useful, so please don't be shy. The shop is open."

Thanking us profusely for our kindness, Arthur walked up to the middle of the bridge, accompanied by Jim, just in case, and went to shout down to their waiting families that all was okay. Meanwhile, Graham started discussing with us what supplies they could do with to make the journey easier.

Food was a priority. We began offloading enough of a variety of both packet and tinned foods to feed the eight of them for an extended period. When asked about weapons, Graham was unsure, because neither he nor Arthur had any knowledge of firearms at all. They'd talked this over and admitted as much to each other.

I insisted, though, that they should take some, and selected two twelve-gauge shotguns. When Arthur returned, I spent a short time showing them both how to handle them safely and how easy they were to use. I didn't allow them to practise firing them, because the noise might attract some unwelcome guests, but I told them that as soon as they were on the river and moving along, they should have a practice and familiarise themselves with them. Chris, one of the later additions to the group, came up with the solution of how to get the growing pile of goods we were creating to the boats easily; to lower it down from the bridge in bags straight onto the decks of the boats.

Maud had already pointed out that there was no point stretching out the chance meeting, as delays wouldn't help either group, so we worked industriously to complete the task of resupplying our new-found friends. In no time we'd loaded the goods onto the trailer Simon was towing, which he drove to the centre of the bridge while we bade farewell to Graham and Arthur, who left, accompanied by Dave, Chet and Jamie to escort them back to the river bank.

Dave handed a hastily written note to Graham, telling him to, at the first opportunity, pass the message on to whoever they found in command. He explained that it contained information about our group, what we'd discovered on our journey, our capabilities and what we hoped to achieve if we found Warwick Castle a suitable long-term shelter.

Half an hour later and sweating with the exertion of lowering bags of goods onto the boats, we waved our final goodbyes over the side of the bridge and continued our journey.

Dave was still ecstatic at the news that some remnants of the British armed forces were still operating, especially his beloved Royal Navy. He was imagining how the fightback would begin as soon as the forces gathering in the Solent combined. Personally, I was overjoyed as well. The plans we'd made and the journey we'd undertaken so far, trying and succeeding to keep my family safe and alive, gathering others along the way, it had all been on the premise that we were doing it alone; that any hope of help from any government and its associated forces had disappeared as the virus spread like wildfire across the globe, eliminating any and all chances of help arriving.

Warwick Castle was planned to be our intended long-term refuge. A place to gather enough supplies and where we could shelter behind its walls until it was safe to emerge into whatever world the zombies left behind, when they hopefully, eventually, rotted away to leave only piles of bones as a reminder of their reign of terror.

An hour and more destroyed undead later, we drove up the motorway exit to join the road that led straight into Worcester. I was now in familiar territory and knew the roads well from my many visits to the small and beautiful city that Worcester had once been. But, even on the outskirts where we stopped, it looked ominous and threatening. Abandoned and crashed vehicles littered the road, many zombies wandered between them now, heading in our direction as the noise of our arrival caught their attention.

The pall of smoke hanging over the city told a similar tale of what we'd witnessed before, and we'd already learned what

Worcester was like from Graham and Arthur's description from when they'd passed through on their boats.

To me it looked too dangerous for us to enter and I could see the concern on Dave's face as he looked ahead. We'd already agreed in principal that we would only try to rescue family and friends if we thought it was safe to do so, but we had made it so far, and the thought of not trying now we were faced with the choice seemed unfair. A case of so near and yet so far.

Was it worth risking all our lives to check, though?

Waiting, looking at what lay ahead, I could only imagine that everyone felt as we in my car did.

Simon was the first to pick up the radio and speak.

"Sorry to say it ,guys, but it looks bloody awful in there. I'm not sure how everyone else feels, but I think it's too risky for us all to try." He paused.

"How about I try? Steve's one of my boys and therefore I'm responsible for him. We promised him we would do this, but it's not worth risking us all. If I unhook my trailer, Steve's already with me to show me the way, the two of us will make the attempt alone. We should be in and out in no time.

Everyone else can stay here and if the zombies get too many, you can all just drive in circles around the motorway island until we return. The radios should stay within range, so we will be in contact."

He chuckled wryly.

"What's the worst that could happen?"

I could have said, "Nothing, apart from you becoming zombie food."

What he was saying made sense. The plans we'd made altered as new situations arose. Initially, we'd chosen to stay together and not weaken the whole by splitting up. That changed when a few of us had gone on the mission from Willie's farm to raid the local gun shop, and when we had divided our forces to attack the ones who'd blocked the motorway and killed Daniel. Both successfully.

Simon was making sense, we owed it to Steve to try, but we also owed it to ourselves not to risk all of us in the process. A one-vehicle, two-man mission would accomplish both of those aims.

He was also not waiting for approval, as he probably knew some of us might try to dissuade him. His mind was made up and he was going, whether we liked it or not. Steve had also made his decision and was already out of the vehicle and unhooking the trailer.

As soon as Steve climbed back into the Land Rover, he took up position on the mounted machine gun and they set off.

Dave chuckled as I sat back down.

"Well, he wasn't leaving that up for debate, was he? Typical Simon. As far as he's concerned, it's his responsibility and he won't put any others in the line of fire, so to speak."

He shrugged, looking out of the window at the approaching zombies.

"Oh well, let's wait for him to come back. In the meantime, I think we should do as he suggests and keep moving, so that little lot approaching won't give us any problems."

Agreeing, I radioed Shawn to get moving and we all formed up behind him and started to drive slowly around the large island that straddled the motorway, adding more to the former zombie count with every revolution. We could hear the occasional distant chattering of the machine gun tracking Simon and Steve's progress as they drove deeper into the dead City of Worcester.

Fifteen minutes later, I was beginning to get concerned because the machine gun hadn't been heard for a while and no updates had come over the radio, and then we received a message from Simon.

They were returning empty handed and asked us to clear any zombies from around the trailer to enable them to hook it back up and get moving without delay.

The message left a lot unsaid, but it didn't really need to say more. Steve's family hadn't made it.

Despite our best efforts, we were still forty-two and two dogs.

EPILOGUE

Once the trailer was hitched, we set off again. We weren't re-joining the motorway, as the route we'd planned followed the A road from the junction we were at, eventually ending up in Warwick. From Worcester, it was the most direct route and the obvious one to pick, with an added advantage that it didn't pass directly through any large towns or villages.

I was back on, if not familiar territory, at least roads I'd driven along before, albeit under less dangerous conditions, and in a normal car instead of in a bastardised armoured version such as I was currently driving. I tried not to get my hopes up too much. The journey we'd started out on what seemed like a lifetime of experiences and weeks ago was drawing to its end.

I had, on the very first day the apocalypse started, sat on Bodmin Moor and said that we needed to get to a castle, as it would be the best place to ensure our survival. Not once, despite meeting more people both accidentally and by design, had we wavered from that goal. Everyone we met agreed with us that it was the best plan.

Now we were nearing that goal. Would it be all we hoped it would and could be? How much of a fool would I feel after encouraging everyone that it was the best place to try to reach, only to find it unsuitable when we got there?

I kept my thoughts to myself, but doubt filled me up to bursting point. Had I led everyone to their deaths when we could have found a safe place without having to endure the hundreds of miles we'd travelled?

Becky had always said I was easy to read: unable to hide my emotions. I always denied it, but knowing there was a reason I was not very good at poker, I took her gentle mocking and poking fun at me when she always saw straight through whatever emotional mask I was trying to put on.

Dave proved this when we were sitting down on a quiet section of the road, as he said, "Tom, don't worry, mate. I have a feeling that this castle we're heading to is going to work out."

I replied wearily, "I don't know. What if I've led us on a wild goose chase and all we find is a fucking nightmare. I hope so too, but the closer we get, the more nervous I am. You've all trusted some stupid idea I had on the first day this began. What if I'm wrong?"

"Nah, mate. You're right. My old bones are telling me so, and sometimes you have to trust your gut. It felt right to you when you first thought of it and it's felt right every time you've mentioned it again." He laughed.

"And anyway, it's a bit fucking late now to change your mind." He pointed to a road sign informing us we were ten miles away from Warwick.

His words helped but didn't lessen how nervous I was feeling. The road provided no obstructions Shawn couldn't deal with using his plough, and we only encountered significant numbers of zombies as we skirted around the famous town of Stratford upon Avon. Not reducing speed, we cleaved through the masses shambling along aimlessly until attracted by our approaching engine noise.

Their futile efforts to stop our passage ending the moment they met tonnes of moving metal. The only reminder of their existence showed in maybe another dent or at the very least, a streak of red gore to add to the others that were building up in layers all over our vehicles.

Passing over the M40 motorway, I knew we were only minutes away from our destination.

I picked up the radio.

"Shawn, we're very close now. I've been here loads of times and always use the main car park. We need to find the service vehicle entrance they use to allow their own vehicles to enter the grounds after hours. It might be a good idea if we do some reconnaissance first to save us driving around until we find it. If you could form a square, I recommend that Simon and I scoot ahead and see what we can find."

After acknowledging and confirming it was a good idea, Simon and I hung back and waited until they had formed an impenetrable mini fortress with the remaining vehicles.

Simon unhitched his trailer once more and we were ready. With everyone standing on the seats, holding weapons ready, we set off. Ending more zombie lives with quiet thrusts of spears or a swing of Jamie's axe, I slowly drove onwards. Not sure of where to try first, I turned off the road, following signs to the main carpark and stopped at the still closed main gates. A padlock held the locking bar closed.

"That's a good sign, I think," Dave muttered quietly. "If it's locked, then there shouldn't be any visitors inside. They didn't have time to open the gates before it hit. Let me see if I can open it. Chet, find the bolt croppers, please, it's time for a bit of breaking and entering."

Taking the bolt croppers, he walked to the gate, quickly inspected the padlock before raising the heavy-duty tool and easily cutting the shackle on the lock. Sliding the locking bar open, he swung one leaf of the gate open, performed a theatrical bow and indicated for us to drive through.

Once through, he closed the gate behind us, ran to the car and quickly scrambled in.

Further up the familiar drive, I noticed a gate in the perimeter fence I hadn't noticed on my visits before. Looking through it, I could see a roadway that led through the grounds.

Bingo! It had to be the one we wanted.

"This looks like a good option, Dave. Same again, mate, if you please."

With another flourish, he opened the gate and waved us through.

Slowly driving through the grounds, I tried hard to contain my excitement. The place looked deserted. Being a major tourist attraction and a site of significant historical importance, it would have a good perimeter fence to dissuade anyone trying to dodge paying the entry fee and to protect it when it was closed. The timing of the virus hitting had, for once, it seemed, worked to our advantage. It was closed when the world changed forever, and it never reopened.

We still needed to be careful, though, I reminded myself. It would surely have security staff on site twenty-four hours a day, and the perimeter fences, though difficult to climb, wouldn't stop someone desperately trying to escape by getting over them.

We rounded the corner, and the castle came fully into view as we continued up the road. Carrying on, and with Simon following closely behind, we passed what I knew was called the Mound. It was the original site of the castle, built not long after the Norman invasion of England in 1066.

The road led straight through a gateway in the main curtain wall. I pulled into the main courtyard, stopped the car and turned the engine off. Standing on the seat as quickly as I could, I looked eagerly around.

Not a soul, living or dead, was in sight.

Simon pulled up beside me and turned off his engine and stood up on his seat as well.

All of us stared in awed silence at what we had discovered.

Simon broke the long silence by turning to me with a huge smile on his face.

"You, Sir, are a fucking genius! Look at this place. It's incredible."

He pointed to the gate we'd just driven through and to another entrance, which I knew in its dark depths was the original fortified barbican protected entrance.

"'If we can get those closed, this place will be impenetrable." Dave joined in, slapping me hard on the back.

"And if we can't close them, we can just brick them up."

I was far too happy to even try to deny the congratulations being thrown in my direction. We had done it against insurmountable odds. From an idea born from desperation, the reality we had made it was hard for me to comprehend fully. Tears ran down my face as my emotions boiled over and I unashamedly shed tears of joy and happiness, until eventually pulling myself together.

"Let's go and get the others," I said.

Fifteen minutes later, forty-two people and two dogs hugged, kissed, cried, laughed and barked in celebration. Number forty-three and forty-four of our group were still to weak to celebrate and lay asleep in the trailer.

We had arrived at our Zombie Castle.

Chris Harris is a UK-based author, well-known for his post-apocalyptic and zombie book series.
Find his website at www.chrisharrisauthor.co.uk
Facebook @chrisharrisauthor

UK Dark Book 1: The Blackout

By Chris Harris

"What would happen if……?"

Many people ask themselves the question, but how many actually do something about it?

Tom lives in Birmingham, England with his family. After asking himself the question and researching what could happen, he decided it wouldn't do any harm to be a little bit prepared. Just in case.

He discovers the world is going to be hit by a massive Coronal Mass Ejection from the sun, which will turn the whole planet dark.

He only has a few days to get ready.

Will they survive?

People want what they have, but is he prepared to kill to protect it?

The UK Dark series, out now!